Beyond my Blinkers

Beyond my Blinkers

Subir Adhicary

Vitasta
LET KNOWLEDGE SPREAD
www.vitastapublishing.com

Published by
Renu Kaul Verma
Vitasta Publishing Pvt Ltd
2/15, Ansari Road, Daryaganj
New Delhi – 110 002
info@vitastapublishing.com

ISBN 978-93-86473-40-0

First Edition 2019
MRP 395

Edited by Sangita Menon
Sketches by Subir Adhicary
Cover and layout by Somesh Kumar Mishra
Printed by Vikas Computer and Printers

Words of Praise

Subir Adhichary's writing is relatable and it feels that it has happened with 'me', the reader also. The beauty of the narrative is its simplicity and depth. The writing transports you into a whirlpool of thoughts and ruminations. Read to transport into a nostalgic world. The writing is like a journey. Enjoy the ride.

Dr Anurag Batra

Chairman, *Businessworld*, entrepreneur, author, tv show host and angel investor

Subir Adhicary has put together some interesting anecdotes from daily life which we normally miss out in the dog-eat-dog race of professional life. These small incidents remind us of life's many facets and how the human mindset works under different circumstances. We are everyday confronted with the proverbial Chauhanji and his do not care attitude who gives us a strong lesson on how everything in life has to be taken in its stride. There are plenty of free loaders like

Batraji who confront us in our day-to-day lives and who make it a virtue to live off others. It was a great reminder of real life and the way we all live it, mostly without noticing it within the nuances of a professional and stressful lifestyle. It refreshed a lot of memories from my life and is a stark reminder of the way life goes on. Adhicary brings the anecdotes to life through a conversational style which helps us relate to the events and identifies them with each one of us. The simple narrative adds to the flavour of the already interesting prose.

Arindam Mukherjee

Editor, *Outlook Money*

Subir Adhicary, a retired engineer, is a multi-talent. I am now discovering his flair for writing, laced with original humour and sharp witticism, like,'...discarded Mahatma Gandhi for other Gandhis. They are doing fine.' These short snippets, on various aspects of life that we all encounter commonly, are often like seeing in a mirror. But he also suggests solutions to our social problems. Reading these would be both fun and a lesson.

DK Jain

IFS, a former ambassador

His pen is more of an honest mirror, ruthlessly showing the worst of the present decadent society with stunning vengeance. He is brilliantly hilarious like PGW and ruefully sarcastic like Harishankar Parsai. Leaves you uneasy and contemplative.

Dr Uday KM

former VC, Arya Bhatta University

Subir Adhicary has painted a wonderful picture of the trials and tribulations of a society with an infectious sense of humour. It shows that laughter is a great reliever of life's inevitable pains and frustrations.

PK Chakraverty, MBE

Her Majesty's Customs Service
(Law Enforcement & Anti-smuggling),
London Airports

To

My

Dronacharyas

RK Narayan, Sardar Khushwant Singh

and Ruskin Bond

whose lucid and prolific writings have

always captivated me

—Ekalavya

and my granddaughter

ADRITA

Contents

Acknowledgements

To write a book is very easy – to get it published is a Herculean task for new authors. More so in the times of e-books and electronic gadgets. Many books, post-printing, occupy warehouse space for years – ultimately getting pulped. Still the craving made me search for a publisher. And I found one where one of my acquaintances had got her book published without much ado. It was VITASTA publishers in Daryagunj. I sent my sample pages and after a week met the ever-smiling Renu Kaul Verma. While waiting for her in her office full of books, I saw a brief for her staff on the board. The first, the good manuscripts were to be given 80% time. Second types with promise were to be actively promoted after taking post-dated cheques. Third types were to be asked for full advance with no risk.

For the fourth type it was 'do not waste time'. I was sure to be in the fourth type. Renuji came in and we discussed the book. A hot cup of tea came in. We discussed for more than 45 minutes and I knew at least I was not in the fourth set.

I thank my wife Ruma for still not believing that I can write – which motivates me, my son Siddhartha who has inherited my genes of jest and writing and my daughter Soma for being my in-house editor and unbiased critic. I also thank my daughter-in-law Ditipriya and son-in-law Debarshi Ray for being the cheerleaders.

I thank Renuji, Ms Papri, Ms Preeti and Someshji for their help in getting the book published. Thanks are also due for my reviewers who took pain to read the manuscript.

A special mention is to be made about Anurag Batra. A man of many talents and one who adorns many hats, Anuragji is one of the youngest media Moghuls, an author, tv show host and Chairman of the iconic *Businessworld* group. Despite his busy schedule, he found time to read my articles, got a few published in his group magazines and encouraged me all through. I remain indebted to him.

I also thank Arindam Mukherjee, Editor, *Outlook Money* magazine.

Preface

I realised that I had the potential to write about the mundane matters of life which we miss and mess – in my own style – at the age of 65. The canvas to write regularly was provided by a dynamic couple, Mukesh Sinha and Sudha Sinha, who publish a weekly newspaper with a circulation of 40,000 called 'Dwarka City'. The paper has been around since 2002. It was a fortnightly until last year and has become synonymous with the bristling sub-city. I was given space to write in it and the independence to write whatever I wanted. The feedback through the last four years from Dwarka's erudite denizens of all age groups was very satisfying, and it emboldened me to write regularly except for periods when I suffered from writer's block.

Dwarka, New Delhi's largest sub-city has a population

of about one million plus. Readers will find it mentioned in this book. It is my 'Malgudi'. A typical Indian City to have developed in the recent times. As ill-conceived as they come. The planning lacks foresight and is bereft of common sense. The residents suffer in nonchalant silence. The place offers enough food for thought. For vultures like me.

I am an unabashed fan of RK Narayan, Sardar Khushwant Singh and the living legend Ruskin Bond. Their styles enabled a reader to meander through their stories without stumbling. The pace and the innate humour never leave the lines of their works.

I have attempted to do the same subconsciously. I have not read Wren & Martin. My attempt is simple – to make people smile and identify themselves with the protagonists in the stories. I would, therefore, request my readers to overlook `how it has been written' and read 'what has been written'. A flicker of a smile on the tired face of a reader would be my greatest reward.

The smell and feel of a printed book are still rare feelings. More so, if the book is your own creation. I, therefore, thought of publishing all my articles in the form of a book. The idea was encouraged by some of my permanent readers, among others.

The Protest Technologist

I love the pungent smell of roasted coffee which wafts out of Barista, CCD and similar outlets. It is ethereal. The cost is, however, jolting, triggered by merciless taxation.

The taxes are nearly as much as the base cost. A case of the seed being bigger than the fruit. So, while hanging out aimlessly, I open the glass doors of the outlets, pretend to look for a prime seat and inhale the fragrance which opens up the clogged avenues of my mind. I know it is unethical. Our texts say – *Ghrahnen ardha bhojanam* which means – to smell food is partly eating it. Given that logic, I should pay at least half the price.

During one such aimless walk, I stood near the doorway of a CCD outlet, fiddling with the door handle and fighting with my conscience, when I felt a gentle tap on my shoulders. Turning around, I saw Batraji, who was my neighbour in a previous locality. He was a modern day Robert Bruce. There is no business that he has not tried albeit with repeated failure. That never deterred him from embarking on to new ventures. Failures are the pillars of success he believed, although his old father, who was unfortunately the ATM for such ventures, did not share his son's view, for his financial pillars were being shaken badly by his enterprising son. My reverie was broken by a nudge from Batraji. 'Aur Sir, coffee-shoffee ho jaye', he said, and literally shoved me into the shop. With great elan he crossed over to a twin seater and beckoned me to join him. He exuded an unlikely radiance and a confident gait. I was impressed and surmised that he must have succeeded at last. I felt happy for his father.

'Aur Sir, kaisa chal raha?' he asked, after ordering two of the most expensive coffees available. 'Bacchhe-shacche kaise hain?' He had this habit of creating rhyming word pairs so common to north India 'chai-shai, khana-peena, ghoomna–shoomna'.

'Passing the days somehow. Bhai, a retired person has all the time at his disposal sans money.'

'Now! Now! Dada do not tell me that. You have no liability now. Bacchon ki shaadi-waadi kar di ki nahin?" I could understand shaadi but not waadi. And how I hate the word 'Dada' used for all Bengalis irrespective of age. So, we have an aged Bappida, Mithunda, Kishorda being addressed as if they had all passed their childhood playing gilli-danda in the alleys with the 'name-callers'.

'Oh yes, that is over,' I said. 'Now, my health is the only liability. But tell me about you. You seem to have got into a profitable business, I see.'

Batra gave me a munificent smile, shrugged, coughed and called the waiter over to order two pastries. Then, he lowered his face and said, 'You are bang on right, Sir. Now, I have a business that is in demand, and I am deeply involved in it.'

'Well, what is it?' I enquired.

'Protest Technology,' he said.

I looked in wonder. Never heard of it. What sort of

business was it? The cup of coffee stayed where it was – midway to my lips. Looking at my perplexed expression, Batra proceeded to explain.

'It is like this, Sir. With the law and order problems, intolerance issues, blame games, questions of who is right and who is wrong, the Indo-Pak jhamela-shamela, You know what I mean…Woh wahan ke gaane-shaane wale ka chakkar, the frequency and style of protests have increased manifold. The media is also highlighting this a lot. The country has big potential for new and cutting-edge protest styles and material'.

'But', I tried to intervene, stuffing a delicious pastry into my mouth.

'Now, there's heavy demand for candles of all sizes and colours. I am trying to import non-flammable, simulated candles for NGOs specialising in protest marches. It is a new concept, from Turkey. Another thing that is in vogue nowadays is throwing ink at people to blacken their face. The victims then stay with blackened faces, until the media calls it a day. Therefore, you need a chemical that lasts at least a day or two and is camera friendly. I mean, it should shine. I am importing such an ink from a South American country famous for such smear protests. Research-wisearch karna parta hai, Sir.'

'What else?', I asked, in disbelief.

'No one wants to lose slippers and shoes just to protest. So, we supply dummy shoes and slippers for throwing or beating. You can order shoe garlands, as well. The latest trend is wearing masks during protests so that one does not get caught later via CCTVs. Ku Klux Klan style, you see. Direct from the USA'. Batraji thumped the table in glee. Robert Bruce Batra had hit the jackpot.

'And, who are the buyers?' I asked.

'Oh! There are many. NGOs whom I call 'Noise Generating Organisations', political parties, fledgling politicians from universities, school students – ab kaun kaun bataun, Sir. I am also tying up with an online selling firm to supply this in retail while I will concentrate on corporate sales. Moreover, we have a legal cell to help people get bail at a nominal cost with full media coverage.' Batraji's mobile rang and he abruptly stood up and walked to the door without even a perfunctory adieu and vanished the way he came.

I sat stupefied, calculating the amount of the bill for the expensive coffee and black forest pastries which I had devoured believing that Mr Protest Technologist would pay for them. How stupid of me! Batra made me pay for my earlier indiscretions of smelling the flavour for free.

I am now thinking of a cutting-edge protest.

Positive Thinking

Nowadays, unfolding a newspaper is a juggler's job. Leaflets of all sizes spill out by the dozen all around you as you try to get to the news. Leaflets promoting a herbal medicine for flawless skin, advertisements for inexpensive blood tests, information on everything from sofa repair to body repair, groceries at 'heavvy discounts', tasty food from 'your kitchen' to 'his kitchen', 'art of living' classes to 'art of leaving' classes, and what not. Once, I saw a leaflet for a course on 'Positive Thinking'. It claimed that you could imbibe positive traits by undergoing just one simple course. Just as I was reading this, I saw Mr Chauhan walking toward me, with a limp. He had joined that course. I was inquisitive about the outcome of such a course. Mr Chauhan was a retired government official whom I had met at a meeting on some sector-related issues. He was critical of everything. He seemed to be a Devil's advocate. Someone in the crowd had suggested to him that he should undergo the Positive Thinking course.

He smiled at me and said, 'Hello bhaijaan! How are you doing?'

'All is well, Sir. But I see that you are limping,' I said.

'I got hit by a rickshaw,' he said. 'But it is a boon,' he added.

'Why is that so?' I asked.

'I do not have to drive now and spend on petrol. I do not have to go for those silly family functions for now I can cite my inability to drive. I get free pick-up and drop as well. Hai na savings, bhaijaan? Think positive!'

'What about your daughter for whom you were looking for a match?'

'Oh! She saved me the trouble and much money by eloping with a guy of her choice. I don't even know their whereabouts. Isn't that wonderful? Think about it! No hassles, no baaratghar booking, no catering expenses, no dowry. I am so happy. Think positive!'

'But, Chauhan Sahab,' I tried hard to find words. 'What about your son?'

'Don't you know? He is in Tihar jail,' Chauhan Sahab said with a glint in his eyes and a broad smile on his face, as if his son has just settled in London or San Fransisco. 'Sentenced for fifteen years on charges of a chit fund scam along with his wife.'

My jaw had dropped to my chest by now. Seeing me bewildered, Chauhan Sahab winked and stated, matter-of-factly, 'See, he is just thirty-five. When he comes out, he will be fifty. Only he knows where he has kept his money. So, he will enjoy when he is released. For now, they are enjoying free accomodation, food, clothing, with Yoga classes and movies thrown in. Lucky guys, no?'

I was stunned and stood in a stupor. Chauhan Sahab shook me, and said, 'Bhaijaan, what happened? Think Positive!'

'And, Bhabhiji?' I stuttered.

'Thankfully, she is bedridden with gout, and can only shout at the top of her voice cursing her luck, rueing the day she got married to me.'

'So, don't you get mad?'

'Oh! Come on, Bhaijaan! Think Positive! Have you seen the menace of pigeons and crows in our society?'

'Yes,' I said, 'and stray dogs.'

'Right, but no one dares to sit and shit on my balcony or verandah. My wife's cacophany ensures that they avoid my place. So, no regular cleaning as others have to do.' 'But then, nights?' I enquired.

'Who cares... with half a bottle of rum inside...and Positive Thinking?'

I felt the course had worked wonders on Mr Chauhan. Nowadays, I am taking the pamphlets quite seriously. I am cleaning my pet's poop with them. That is Positive Thinking!

Left is always Right

Of late, the Delhi government has come up with a very innovative (?) idea to curb corruption in government offices. The government asks citizens to 'Record the demand of bribe made by the person and send it to a particular number with the assurance that he will be put behind bars. Bravo! Most of us must have confronted such demands to facilitate work at (n)ever burdened government offices. The person asking for it never asks that loudly. It is either in gestures or in a voice that is hardly audible to those around him. These people generally avoid eye contact. It is nearly impossible to capture anything on phone. So, it appears that during the last two months, the population of Tihar has not grown. And, by the way, is voice proof considered admissible for conviction? The initiative is laudable, but the means are not.

It reminds me of a marketing blitz way back in the sixties. An advertisement in leading newspapers came out promising certain death to bedbugs. As the contraption was imported, buying time was short. There was a big scramble to buy the same. It did arrive after a few days through VPP. On opening the nicely packed box, out came two wooden strips with an instruction that read 'Catch the bug, put it on one of the strips and crush with the other strip!'

I had joined the Uttar Pradesh Irrigation department in 1974 as a sub-divisional officer. Fresh out of college, I was full of self respect, honesty and a craving to do something for society. It was a foolish vision. The department had water tight rules for commission. Every contract had a fixed percentage that would be sought quietly. The bribe was for everyone, from peons to ministers. We had three types of officers – Acchaa (good), Chant (clever) and Bewaqoof (fool). Acchaa took his percentage without fuss and did the work. Chant took the percentage but harassed the briber for more. Bewaqoof did not take any money and was scorned by all. The census was 50% good, 45% chant and 5% bewaqoofs. Bewaqoofs were either given design and planning or shunted out to Godforsaken places.

Though being branded Bewaqoof, I stoically defended my vision for two years. The final straw came when my travelling bill of Rs190 was not passed. On inquiring after a couple of months, I was told by my clerk that the accountant wanted 10% or Rs19. 'Arre kauwa kabhi kauwe ka gosht khata hai?' I refused to pay, and the bill came back to me with comments in red, scribbled all over it. It still lies unpaid in my archives. I left my Gazetted job in disgust. Some of my enlightened friends stayed back, shrugging off the burden of self respect, debt to motherland, and so on, which were infused in us at the university and discarded Mahatma Gandhi for other Gandhis. They are doing fine. Their personal growth rate was much higher than that of our country, thanks to their good stature.

I joined a premier Research Institute in Mumbai. I thought that would be a clean place. Hard luck. It specialised in Travelling Expense and Research grant fudging. Top to bottom. And, all respected scientists. Then, I joined a family-held private company. I was posted at a tunnelling project in Himachal Pradesh. Family held and private. Corruption should have been miles away, logically. The myth was shattered during the very first weekend. I was asked to counter-sign a muster roll of workers which contained more than the deployed numbers. I protested. I was threatened by the labour zamadar. My superiors, for whom the inflated bills were made, naturally asked me to cooperate and sign. The site was remote, the tunnel was 6.5 kms long and River Tons meandered along the site. I was too young to die unsung. I gave in, signed and left the job after a few months of a constrained existence.

Corruption is not a tumor that can be operated upon and cured. In our country, it is a Cancer. Only transfusion can mitigate the evil. The mindsets have to change – of the taker and of the giver. Huge social imbalance, massive gaps between haves and have nots and limitless craving for riches have all together clouded our psyche. This has been fanned by the rich to get an easy way out by enticing officials in authority with bribes or facility money. Bribing existed earlier, too, and was called 'Utkoch'.

Corruption has permeated all over. We have to fight it rationally. Starting from value education at the school level. By exemplary acts. By shunning socially corrupt people. This cannot be achieved overnight. Time will come – slowly and decisively. Until that moment, the left hand will remain stronger than the right hand. Tucked under the table… in anticipation.

Snakes and Ladders

ACT I

Tyagiji is morose today. Never in his dreams had he seen this coming. He had been on the edge for the last week or so – not stepping out of his house unless someone was home. He stocked up Limca and some snacks. He instructed the society guards appropriately. He kept his drawing room clean and arranged. And, he wore clean and crisp clothes. He listened quite intently to every footstep in the corridor. He regularly checked with the guards whether anyone was looking for him. But no one came.

Diwali came and went, leaving behind polluted air and heaps of burnt crackers. Tyagiji could not sleep all night. He tossed around, thinking of the gifts that were coming his way. Dry fruits, kaju barfis, dinner sets, toasters, mink blankets and even gold or silver coins. Nothing arrived. He had retired a few months ago after serving in a senior position and had been getting gifts since the gifting system gripped the festival during the late seventies or so. During Diwali, he never used to leave his seat or cabin, and he did not take leave, lest the gifts were missed. His wife used to keep clean dry containers ready to be filled up with the gifted dry fruits. And, the mixers, toasters, vases received were conveniently given away as gifts that were rewrapped to unsuspecting relatives on different occasions. This year, it was a big let down. Tyagiji could not reconcile to the fact that the gifts were not for him, but for his chair, which now belonged to someone else. He sunk his face into the pillow in self pity. Tears rolled down his cheek.

ACT II

I saw Misraji feeding eatables to the stray dogs in the service lane near his society. He loved feeding stray dogs. He was a friendly neighbour who had retired a few years ago from a private firm. He stayed in a two-bedroom flat with his wife. His son, a management graduate from IIM, stayed in Dubai with his wife and a small kid. Having spent most of his earnings on his son's education, Misraji lived frugally. The couple spent their time taking part in nearby temple kirtans and watching TV. I walked up to him to exchange Diwali greetings, and enquired about their absence from the society get-together.

'Oh, just like that. Your Bhabhi was not feeling well, and these crackers,' he blurted, looking sideways. I could sense something amiss. 'What has happened, bhaisaheb? Is everything alright?' I queried. 'And, all these sweets and namkeens you are feeding these dogs?' I was puzzled. Misraji looked at me, and with a tinge of sadness in his voice, said, 'Bhai, your Bhabhi had made these with her own hands for Guddu, spending hours despite her arthritic condition. We were hoping to meet them after two years. Our grandson is four years old now, and we were looking forward to hug him, play with him and cuddle him.' He paused, looked up to the sky, and continued, 'But last week Guddu called and expressed his inability to come, as they are going on a European tour instead'. Well. They had been doing so for the last two years. He offered to send some money which I refused. Arey, we are only two people. I can pull on. These dogs are always with me, winter, summer or monsoon. So, I gave the sweets to my kids here. Thik kiya na?' Misraji feigned a laugh but I could see tears welling up in the corners of his eyes. Flustered, he wiped them, and said, before turning away, 'Too much smog. Cannot stand it.' He walked off, shoulders drooping, defeated by life.

P.S.: Look around. You will find several Tyagijis and Misrajis. All defeated by the system or by their own blood. Life is sometimes cruel. Like a game of Snakes and Ladders.

—AT LEAST GET OFF MY BACK NOW

The Fat Weddings

You have not lived your life if you have not attended a highend marriage ceremony in Delhi. Call it boisterous, ostentatious, cacophonous or dhamakedaar (explosive), one is simply awestruck by the scale, the grandeur and the flamboyance of such weddings. The invitation comes with a box of sweets, cookies or dry fruits with a thick pack containing a card or cards, depending upon the closeness of the relationship, encompassing a spectrum of functions. On the day of the marriage, you have to navigate traffic jams to reach the venue; late by hours, and with ruffled nerves. However, in most cases, the groom's party never reaches before midnight, dancing to the tunes of 'aaj mere yaar ki shaadi hai' or 'yeh chauri chhaati veeron ki'. Brass bands in Roman attire with outstretched hands reach out to grab the notes waved by Phuphajis and Mamajis.

The ladies, in glittering attires – even in temperatures of four degrees, valiantly display 80% of their body mass. The final journey of the groom takes hours to reach the venue, at the most three hundred metres away, by which time you would have partaken a range of snacks (read snakes) before moving on to the main courses which would include Chinese, Italian, South Indian, Rajasthani and North Indian dishes to say the least. In most weddings, you may finish dining, hand over the envelope with the gift money, and citing the distance problem, slink away without even seeing the groom or the bride. I am describing the kind of people you come across during such weddings.

Dedicated: You can identify these people, generally Mamajis (maternal uncles), Chachajis (paternal uncles) and Brothers, by their disheveled countenance, hasty entry and exits and lost looks. They are the ones who make all the arrangements – from the decoration to the departure. Do not expect more than a fleeting smile or a nod from them. They are the ones who manage the crowd, its eccentricities and tantrums.

Ladycated: Those of this category put on their best attire, wear costly perfumes, flash gold chains, and are mostly found within a radius of one meter from the ladies. They dance fitfully tripping over the women, trying to get everyone's attention by performing the 'snake dance', twists, shakes and every other conceivable dance move. They approach women with a fixed smile and gladly fetch snacks for them all the while ogling them. They attend marriages for this simple pleasure of life, so you should not give them more than a look and let them have their fun.

Medicated: This main category believes in the pleasures of the bottle. It frequents marriages for a few good pegs of generously served Single Malt (read Molt). After a few pegs, such men become 'too-generous' and overtly friendly. If a woman is approached by someone who repeatedly enquires about whether she has eaten or not, be certain that the man belongs to this category. The hardened ones do not sway

– the initiated ones do. Disgruntled Phoophajis – deprived of in-law's properties, friends, rejected lovers and distant cousins form a majority in this category. They hardly reach the dinner area because by then they are lost to the world, soaking in the joys of the ceremony through liquid pleasure.

So, look out for the next marriage season, and watch carefully. You will definitely enjoy.

Testing Times

I met Amal babu in the Sector 6 market last week. He looked ruffled and drained and was not at his chirpy best. He stays in Kolkata and occasionally comes here to do nanny sitting for his grand daughter. One of his qualities is that he never gives his listeners a chance to talk or revert like a popular TV anchor on a prime-time debate that we all know. That evening in March he was inexplicably defused. I had to prod him to know the reason. He had developed a small but painful boil on his groin. Like most vintage Bengalis, he was on homeopathic medicines but his son-in-law insisted that he consult a allopathic doctor. Unfortunately, the doctor had a nursing home, and he immediately dispatched Amal babu there for numerous tests and treatment. So, after a couple of days there, the boil dried up. Along with it, dried up his wallet too. The pain of such a cash drain for a minor boil was more than the pain he was enduring physically. I sympathise with him. It is now common to undergo tests for ailments that you may not be suffering from but to pretend to eliminate the possibility of such an ailment and to correctly diagnose it.

Two places that I fear to tread to are the motor mechanic's garage and nursing homes. You go to these places with one specific problem and they invent or discover ten others. Some months ago, I had noticed a strange metallic sound in my car. I went to a nearby garage. Even as I had just begun to expound on the problem, the mechanic had grabbed the car keys from me, shoved me aside, and had raced off with my car. He was out of sight for about twenty minutes as I stood helplessly calculating the amount of petrol he was wasting at Rs 65 a litre. Then, I noticed my car zooming in like a fighter plane, and out came the grave pilot aka mechanic. He wore a serious look and opened up the bonnet. 'But the sound is from the rear,' I protested. He ignored me. In a short time, half the car parts under the bonnet lay scattered. After doing this striptease job, he grinned and said, 'Aap bach gaye, sahib (You have escaped, Sir). There are a lot of problems.' The cost of such an escape, after the repair was over, was quite substantial. The guru with his three Mobil-smeared chelas carried out their research on my car for about three hours while I watched them in utter resignation, seated under the shade of a Jamun tree, sipping sugar laden 'ispesaal' chaay, a freebie. I swore never to return. The sound still persists.

Last year, during an inspection of a building in Jalandhar, I tripped down the stairs. I hurt my ribs. Being a Sunday, most clinics were shut. So, I was taken to a nursing home. It was no less than a four-star hotel. It had an imposing foyer and a couple of receptionists sat there dressed up as if they were to go to a reality show. Soon, a manager in impeccable dress joined them. They all seemed to be eyeing me as a butcher eyes a goat. A lengthy form was required to be filled. Most columns pertained to my economical status rather than my physical condition. I could see a glitter in the eyes of the manager when I ticked the 'Yes' box for mediclaim eligibility. I was immediately wheeled into a medical room full of modern contraptions and given a painkiller. Later, a young doctor came in, eyes puffed from his afternoon siesta and proceeded to examine me. After checking everything except the affected part, he ordered me to put on my shirt. He occupied his chair with a grave face. 'Are you an alcoholic?', he asked. 'No chance', I replied. 'Then, you must be a heavy smoker,' he queried. 'No, Sir. I do not smoke,' I replied. By then, the pain in the rib had become unbearable. The doctor looked at me solemnly, like a judge delivering a life sentence, and pronounced, 'You have to be admitted. We have to carry out some tests tomorrow.' I protested. 'But why?' I asked. 'Well, you have a sluggish liver, hydro nefritis, hypertension and possibly gastritis,' he responded. 'But, what about my pain?' I nearly yelled. '! Oh that? It's only a minor bruise. We have given you a painkiller and a sedative,' he said yawning. So, after ten unnecessary tests, and poorer by a few thousands, I forced my way back to Delhi after three days. What a fall that was! The pain recurs sometimes reminding me of the 'nursing hotel'.

I am prompted to write this as I came across a news item in *The Times of India* regarding the growing commercialisation of medical care. There are shocking revelations by numerous whistleblower doctors, which find mention in a well-read report by SATHI (Support for Advocacy and Training to Health initiatives) to highlight the lack of regulation of the sector. The Delhi government is also bringing in a law to check these unnecessary tests and to prevent overcharging.

Until that law is enacted, I have decided to visit clinics with crumpled and old clothes, declaring myself near insolvent, and vowing never to disclose my medi-claim status.

The Changeover

Mughalsarai Junction. The name evoked memories of our yearly visits to Calcutta. For, it was a busy junction where the trains stopped for a while for engine and crew change. It also had the best samosas on the route and equally good tea to go with. Situated half way between Delhi and Calcutta, on Sher Shah Suri Marg or Grand Trunk Road, it was a halting place for the Mughal Armies in the numerous Serais. Hence, the name.

The station came up much later. Soon, the name would be a thing of the past. It is being changed to Pandit Deen Dayal Upadhyay Junction. The link – Deen Dayalji was found dead under mysterious circumstances in the Mughalsarai yard in 1968, about forty-nine years ago. Hence the need to immortalise the Jan Sangh icon. The agenda – well, this is not a political write-up, delving into that subject. It is apparent to all.

The Home Ministry has approved the proposal received from the UP government, and an NOC from agencies such as IB, GSI, CID and the Railways has been obtained. Panditji was born near Mathura. About fifteen institutes, airports and colleges, including a railway station, are already named after him.

A very bright student, he chose politics as a career, and was a co-founder of the Jan Sangh, along with Shyamaprasad Mukherji and others. There is no second opinion on his credibiilty and to his contribution to a party which rules India. This is as if one is following Mayawati's zeal of renaming – albeit Mughal names. The British have been tackled by the earlier ruling party. So, the Sixth Mughal, Aurangzeb, was sent packing from New Delhi, a year ago. To a common man bereft of party affiliations, naming new projects coming up all over, after the icons, is a more prudent idea than trying to rewrite history. That too, in an obvious manner. The present name board of the station has black letters on a yellow background. Hope the background color is not changed. Incidentally, our late Prime minister, Shastriji, was born in Mughal Sarai. How come no one thought of his name? Obvious again.

Soaked in reverie about Mughal Sarai, I doze off, and see the following dream, which I share with my readers. As usual with my dreams, this sequence, too, has no relation to people living or dead, place or time; and any resemblance, if at all, is purely co-incidental.

'Mr George, an IAS officer with an acerbic tongue, and presently the home secretary of the State of Indraprashtha, was packing up his briefcase to go home to have a steaming plate of idli-sambhar after a hectic day when the phone rang. It was a hot line. Directly connected to the CM's home. Mr George picked up the phone. The personal secretary to the Chief Minister, Tewari, was on the other side. George detested the man. He held sway over the CM and was a buffer. 'Good evening, Sir,' he said. 'There is an urgent meeting. Saheb wants you here. The Home Minister and

Deputy CM saheb are also coming,' he said, and hung up. Mr George, cursing under his breath, called his PA, and went out to his white ambassador, waiting in the porch. He directed the driver to go to the CM's residence. The PS had not told him about the agenda of the meeting and George began thinking of everything possible. He could surmise that it was an important meeting as the Deputy CM, a sworn rival of the CM, and the ever-obliging Home Minister Sandeep Langotiya, would be there, too. The Home Minister's weakness for the opposite sex earned him his Langotiya title. The Deputy CM had an eye for the coveted post of the CM and contradicted him on all points. He survived due to his proximity to party bosses and his fund raising capabilities.

The car entered the CM's residence and the secretary was ushered into the drawing room. The CM sat on a three-seater, occupying most of it, while the others sat on the single seaters flanking him. The Chamcha PS was standing behind the CM and Mr George took a seat after exchanging pleasantries. Tea and pakoras on that rain-soaked day were laid out on the center table. The mood in the room was relaxed and the tense secretary also set himself loose. He had to control his statements, he thought to himself. His off hand remarks offended many, including the Dy CM. Picking up a cup of tea, the CM took a sip, looked intently into the home seceretary's eyes, and said, 'Independence Day is on the anvil, Mr George.' The home secretary replied, 'Yes, Sir. We are taking all precautions to have it pass off smoothly. Your venue is being triple sanitised.' The secretary was cut off mid-response. 'Wait. Wait! That is routine stuff. I want real Independence,' said the chief minister. Quite confused, the secretary asked, 'From whom, Sir?' Grinning from ear to ear, the rotund CM said, 'From the past rulers of this beloved country, the oppressors, the looters… I mean the Mughals, the Britishers, the Suris.' The secretary interjected, 'They are all gone now, Sir. I do not follow you'. He was perplexed.

'Yes. I know,' the chief minister replied. 'I intend to rename the roads, the forts, the edifices that bear their names. These will now bear of Indian leaders,' he announced. 'But they also ruled and are ruling, Sir,' countered the home secretary, adding, 'Regarding looting, however, you all know better though.' George's reply was offensive, as usual. The CM and the others were silent for a while. Then, the chief minister said, 'Indian leaders are not rulers. They are servants of the masses. I think you ought to know this, Mr Secretary.' George fumbled with his reply when better sense prevailed. The Chief Minister continued, 'You know that the neighbouring State has marched ahead of us by renaming an important station. The party is very upbeat about it. Therefore, on the occasion of seventy years of our Independence, I propose to rename seventy places. Time is short. So, I would like you to make a list of places bearing the names of the earlier rulers and their satraps and replace them with the names that Tewariji has.' The secretary kept quiet while the deputy CM spoke for the first time. 'Lekin, Mukhyamantriji, you have not taken any names from me to include in the list?' He sounded upset.

The CM cast a long look at him and then said to the dozing home minister, 'The Party has approved the list. You and I do not matter,' 'Sir?' the home secretary asked. 'Do you have some specific names of locations that you would like to change?' he asked. The CM looked at Tewariji. 'Well. There is Qutab Minar, which can be changed to Jaichand Minar, Lodhi Gardens to Porus Gardens, and so on,' Tewariji said, looking at the list.

The home secretary was aghast. His mind, that of a bureaucrat, that of an officer of the Indian Administrative Service, was not registering this. 'Hope you understand it now. Just match names with similar traits if possible,' the CM advised. He added, 'and, Yes, remember that my grandfather, the great freedom fighter, Babu Faqir Chand, is also on the list. He will need a central place, a prime location.' At this, the deputy CM nearly jumped out of his seat, and said, 'But it is said that he was running with a bag stolen from a man in the mob when he was caught and imprisoned.' The CM was livid. 'Who says that? That was a canard spread by the man he looted. I mean, his rival. He even had his arm broken in prison while the Non-cooperation Movement was going on.' The deputy CM laughed. 'It is said that he tripped from the toilet stairs in the prison. Indeed, a real freedom fighter,' he jeered.

Now the home minister intervened. 'Let us have no more fresh controversies at this point. As the CM says, this has the Party's approval. So, Mr George, Do you have any suggestions for a central location to place Faqir Chandji?' The home secretary racked his brain, and said sarcastically, in his inimitable way, 'Sir, to have a good location and similarity, I would suggest Humayun's Tomb. Humayun also did nothing for Hindustan and fell to death from a stair. Perfect similarity. We can rename it Faqir Chand ka Maqbara or Faqir's Tomb.'

The room fell silent. The swarthy complexioned CM's face became violet with blood rushing to it. Red when mixed with black produces a violet colour. Only the deputy CM was stifling a laugh.

It is not sure whether the renaming will take place before 15 August. However, Mr George, the powerful home secretary's post has been renamed with immediate effect He is now secretary of the newly constituted Ministry Of Garbage Collection and Disposal.

P.S.: The Mughal army that used to take a break at Mughal Sarai consisted more than eighty per cent of Indian soldiers. Rajputs, Kolis, Maratha merceneries. So, the premises of change are unfounded.

The Jugaad

During the past forty-four years of my career, I have come across all sorts of people. Honest and dishonest, prankies and crankies, straight and crooked, right and dull, et al. Each has contributed to the pages of my book of life. I have watched them, grown with them, imbibed or abhorred their qualities, making me emerge stronger in the game of Snakes and Ladders called career. I remember a few incidents which have helped me survive, later in life.

June 1973. I had just completed my Engineering degree from the University of Roorkee. The results were still awaited. The job scene was depressing. The UP government was in a financial crisis and development works were on hold. Pan India, private intake was low. So, before leaving for home, I met our Head of Department, Dr OP Jain and sought his blessings. Dr Jain was a Civil engineering icon and his students occupied the highest posts all over. He asked me to meet Mr A C Chaturvedi, the then Chief Engineer of UP Jal Nigam (then known as LSGED).

The Chief used to sit in Lucknow, and on a hot afternoon, I met him with Dr Jain's missive. He was very kind and told me that there was no regular vacancy. But respecting Dr Jain's words, he was going to 'adjust' me as a trainee Assistant Engineer at a monthly salary of Rs 250 per month, which was about half the pay of a regular engineer. I readily agreed. Money was not the consideration. It was the engagement, and the job was in Lucknow, the city where I grew up.

I got my first posting at the storm water pumping facility near the historical Residency along the banks of River Gomti. The Junior engineer attached to me was one DR Singh, a wily, hardened Thakur from Gorakhpur. He was not happy to see a young man, fresh from college as his senior. His body language was clear. As I was appointed by the Chief, he was reluctant to take me on. The site was very near the River bank colony which housed senior government officials.

Our Superintending engineer Mr Gupta stayed there. The site fell on his way to the office. So, it was routine for him to stop for a while on the way and check the status, without alighting from the car. He resembled a bloodhound and behaved like one. His white ambassador sent everyone scurrying for cover. He was always in a foul mood in the morning. Perhaps his wife didn't feed him breakfast. I am not sure what the JE told him but he started firing at me from Day Two. He was very rude. As he shouted, I looked at the cannon blasted tower of the Residency and thought about the pounding the British had suffered at the hands of the mutineers of 1857.

My grand Roorkee University ego and self respect were blasted but I stood firm and took it all in my stride. My indifferent attitude made him more furious. A few days passed. I became friendly with Singh. He had, by then, gauged me and was certain that I was more interested in Hazratgunj and plays than getting after him. He felt bad about the badmouthing by the SE. He devised an idea. He knew that the SE. was very fond of meetha paan from a particular shop in Chowk. 'Adhicary Sir,' he said, 'Are you ready to spend Rs2.50 per day to get rid of this man?' I calculated. It was about 25% of my daily earnings. Mutton Biriyani at the Burlington hotel cost Rs10 a plate. Still, I thought it was worth it. And, I agreed, not even knowing why this was required.

The next morning at 10am, the dreaded white Ambassador pulled in. The SE rolled down the window pane as usual and his hound-like mouth opened to spew muck. At this point, Singh, with the gracefulness of a courtier in the Nawab's Durbaar, stretched out his hand. It held a packet. 'Sir, Aap ke liye – gulkand bhi hai, sahab. Naush farmaien.' He said all this with extreme humility. The open mouth stayed open and turned into a grin, which soon vanished as he placed the paan in his mouth very carefully as if placing a baby in a cradle. Then, his eyelids shut down in pure ecstasy. When he opened his eyes after a moment, they bulged out again to fire me. This time, however, no words flew out. He could not afford to throw the paan and fire me. The car glided towards the office. The SE was silenced. This became our routine. The paan stopped his verbal onslaught. He only waved his fingers, and gestured with bulging eyes, which we took in our stride. I later treated Singh with Gymkhana club Kebabs and Ulte tawe ka parantha. We became pals for as long as I stayed at that site. I was subsequently absorbed into the UP PWD. That, of course, is another story.

DR Singh taught me how to find the raw nerve in your boss and press it to your advantage. Try that out at your workplace. All the best.

The Interview

The interview with the Chief Engineer, PDA, was scheduled for 2.30pm, just after lunch. It was after a long follow up that he had agreed to an interview.

He had assumed office a couple of months ago and had been occupied getting acquainted with his fiefdom.

I arrived at the office complex fifteen minutes before time. The lunch timings were 1pm to 2pm but the complex was almost deserted. The staff was outside the gates, busy with post lunch politics. I proceeded to the Chief's office and entered the PA's cabin, a small one. The PA was busy on his mobile phone, completely oblivious to the world. He was in his late fifties. He wore thick glasses, set in a black frame, and he was slightly bald. Presently, he yawned, put down his phone, and looked at me enquiringly. 'I have an appointment with Chief Sa'ab,' I said. 'Is he in there?' I asked. 'Achcha. Ahcha. So, you are from Troubled Times? For that interview?' he asked. I nodded. 'Sa'ab will be late. He has gone to the main office,' he said. 'But he will be here in half an hour or so. Please have a seat.' So, I settled down on the sofa and tried to go through the old PDA brochures lying there.

The cooler behind me rattled like an old helicopter. People peeped in, made enquiries and left at regular intervals. Time ticked on until there was a flurry of movement outside. The PA stood up and looked at the door expectantly. The Chief came in shortly, followed by his staff, files tucked under armpits, and a few hangers on. As is usual with government officials, he walked straight, avoiding eye contact with the people around. The PA and staff followed him into his room, while the hangers on stayed back in the PA's room. I was ushered in after a while. The Chief engineer sat behind a huge table. He was a short, podgy man with a round face accentuated by big bulging eyes. There were a few chairs across the table and his staff stood about them. The Chief, assuming a serious countenance, offered me a chair and motioned the others to sit down. Well, I had an important meeting, you see. A lot of responsibilities of this post, you see.' No apologies for being late. They are not given to apologies. There were no files on the table. I was to take a picture, too. So, I asked him to get some files. 'Oh no! People will think that I do no work,' he said. 'Sir, if there is no file, the Director Sa'ab could presume that you have no work, and further load you,' one staff member suggested. 'Right, Right, give me some files,' the Chief concurred, and stroked his hair. 'Start the interview,' he ordered. I shot out my first question.

'Sir, there have been many irregularities here in the recent past, and it was assured that a relatively cleaner officer would be posted in his position. How do you fit in, Sir?'

'Well, you see,' he cleared his throat. 'I am one of the cleanest. I have only twenty-two ongoing cases against me. Others are far ahead of me. So, Director Sa'ab posted me here.'

'And, what kind of cases, Sir?'

'The kinds that we have. See, if you stand in a drain, the muck will definitely stick to you.' He looked around to elicit reactions from his staff, who nodded approvingly.

'Sir, many flats that were constructed by the PDA have developed distress within a few years. What do have you to say about that?'

'A building is never complete. By the time you construct the top floor, distress starts at the foundation. That is why the maintenance division is started even before the construction starts. The allotted budget has to be finished within the year, you see.' Content with his answer, he again looked at his ever-nodding staff.

'Well, Sir, our town had the best roads. Without potholes and craters. During the last few years, you have allowed nearly every agency to dig trenches along and across. Neither do they repair the roads nor do you. Optical fibre, internet providers, what not. Why do you not repair that?'

'The provisions are for the residents. We will repair once the entire road width is dug up. Then, we can treat it uniformly. Until that point, we leave it like it is. For today, it is Jio, tomorrow, it could be Maro', he said, and burst out into a guffaw, and was joined by his staff.

By this time, the peon had brought in samosas, sweets and tea for everyone.

'What about the CSR activities, Sir?,' I queried. The Chief was perplexed. He looked at me quizzingly.

'Corporate Social Responsibilty – PDA's contribution to the upliftment of the down trodden,' I explained.

'Oh! That! We do have indirect CSR or whatever. We provide steel railings which are regularly stolen by the downtrodden and sold by them to sustain themselves. And, you see our own people. They used to come on cycles. Within years, they have moved over to cars. They all have big kothies. All our CSR, you see.'

'Are you doing anything about the encroachments?' I asked.

'That is the problem. On the one hand, you want us to help the downtrodden, and on the other hand, you want us to dislodge the poor by depriving them of their livelihood. So, what do we do?'

'The encroachments in the PDA colonies and main markets?'

'Oh that? We plan to cover that by taking some fee. It will not be covered area or plinth area. It will be GAO – Grab and Own area.' Ha! Ha! Ha! His eyes closed in self satisfaction.

The mobile rang abruptly. He stood up. 'Director Sir is calling me to his office'. Looking at me, he said, 'Sorry, Sir. I have to rush. Some other day maybe.'

'Sir, your samosas?' the PA asked.

'Pack kardo. Mere aur madam ke liye,' he said, hurrying out. The staff ran after him. I sat with the plate of samosas all alone until the PA came in to pack them along with the sweets. The interview was over.

The Ill Advisors

I dread falling sick. Ever since my childhood, I have a very rich history of falling ill. Bouts of migraine, spells of typhoid, recurrent sinus, kidney stones, gall stones, fractures, bypass surgery, angioplasty, and many a times, PUO (pyrexia of unknown origin) – the name given to a fever which makes doctors clueless. I do not dread the pain, the confinement or the absence of good food. I dread unsolicited advice. This is advice coming from all quarters – from the poncchawali to the neighbours and well-wishers. All sorts of remedies starting from the days of the Ashwini brothers to Hahnemann to modern medicines. The latest addition is Yoga and meditation. One cannot escape the generous counsel of visitors, who drop in to have a peek at your confined condition. They then sip tea and munch namkeens right in front of your starved self.

Last week, I went to see a cousin, who at a young age, has contracted problems in the kidneys and liver. To top it, he is a diabetic. Naturally, the family is alarmed. He has undergone multiple tests at the best hospitals and has been diagnosed properly. Given my Rana Sanga status of sickness, he called me over to discuss the prognosis. I met a crestfallen man and a grave-looking family. Natural, I thought. The reports were encouraging though. He was on the right path to recovery and they knew it. However, it was not the illness but the stream of timely and untimely visitors and their unsolicited and immature advice that was taking a toll on the family. One well wisher even went to the extent of advising that the property and bank deposits be transferred in the name of his wife to avoid legal complications later. And those sitting there nodded in approval while gobbling down rasagollas. The family went into depression and had to be counselled out of it.

These so-called 'advices' come in many forms. You are told about all the food that you must avoid. Invariably, they would include things you like. You could be ticked off because you made the mistake of choosing the 'wrong' doctor or hospital. 'Oh! Ho! Dr Mitra? He spoilt my brother-in-law's uncle's case. He just could not diagnose.' Or, 'Wahan bharti huye? Arre, khatam kar denge. Bas mat pucho. Mere saali ke sasurji' and so on and so forth. Deep exhalations follow thereafter, making one shudder at the prospect. The counsel could also come in the form of the advantages of anulom-vilom or of meditation with a mini demonstration, by the bedside. The parting shot, after polishing off snacks and tea 'that were not necessary' would be, 'OK. Take care. Just give him lauki juice and some vegetable stew, bhabhiji. He will be alright. Call me, if needed.' Rest assured that this person will not be seen unil you fall ill again.

In 2004, I experienced sudden chest pain and visited a prominent hospital. An angiography was carried out, and due to multiple blockage, a bypass was recommended. I was admitted immediately, and the operation was planned the next morning. As the news reached my friends, and family circles, there was a constant stream of visitors – anxious, concerned, surprised; of all sorts. I was cheerful as it was one more routine hospital jaunt for me. The doctor's team was also confident and assuring. Then, at about 9pm, arrived a close family friend with his wife. He looked around the room and declared it was too stuffy. He then proceeded to say in a conspiratory tone that the hospital was not okay for such a major operation. He suggested I opt for a better hospital. A list of failed cases were blurted out to me and to my stunned and petrified wife. They left – mission caution accomplished – with a forced 'Best of Luck' thrown from the door. The night thereafter was terrible. His words haunted me. Sleep came slowly. Fourteen years have passed since the Devil's Advocate counselled me against the hospital. I dread these blinkered advisors – not the sickness.

Now, I invariably tell people that I am alright even if I am unwell. The person asking about my welfare can then just offer a shy smile and say – 'achcha?' The conversation ends there. Topic closed. I now look forward to advising the infirm. Must I not seek revenge for the past sixty-eight years of unwarranted advice?!

Article 377

There has been a raging debate on Article 377 for a while now. The matter has now been settled by the Hon'ble Supreme Court Of India. Regarding the decriminilisation of a colonial act enacted in 1861 and covering forty-two former British colonies. The prohibition of homosexual acts is provided for in section 377 of the penal code. With the passage of time and changed social values, the act is irrelevant now. There are groups and individuals proclaiming their preferences in the open. Socially prominent people are coming out to confess their choice of partners. I was reading the other day that IIT Delhi has allowed a gay forum in the campus. Homosexuality is not a social taboo anymore. Article/Section 377 is debated openly. No eyebrows are being raised. The Dean, IIT Delhi, says that the institute does not differentiate between students on the basis of sexual orientation.

However, in the seventies, the scene was different. Homosexuals or lesbians and gays were socially ostracised and hated. It is not that people did not indulge in such relationships. It was a very private affair, close to the individuals indulging in the act. I am tempted to recount an incident from my engineering college days during that period. Our college was in an industrial town of West Bengal. It had students from all over India. Though our college had a very intelligent, cosmopolitan student composition, it had its share of blinkered and narrow minded ones, too.

An incident related to homosexuality still haunts me as it completely shattered a bright career and a family.

There was one student from Delhi in the fourth year, who was highly suspected to be a homosexual. He was a decent guy, who would help poor students by giving out generous loans, not expecting them to be paid back. He kept to himself, an introvert being, with few friends. The Bengali students in his class and hostel despised him and never left a chance to ridicule him.

He was kept under surveillance for a considerable period by his hostel mates, and one evening, he was caught in a compromising position with a mess boy.

All hell broke loose after that. He was dragged out of the room, mercilessly beaten up, his clothes were torn, and a barrage of obscenities were delivered.

He was then led by a procession of elated students to the Principal's residence, all the while being shoved, beaten and slapped. However, his face betrayed no emotion. He walked stoically, eyes fixed distantly, as if he had done nothing wrong.

The procession became larger and more vociferous by the time it reached the Principal's residence.

One could see the Principal blushing while several students narrated the episode, clamouring for the rustication of this student. Our Principal had spent a considerable amount of time in Britain, and was an open-minded person, far ahead of the times. He counseled that the trait was a sickness, and that it must be handled with compassion. But the mob was not in a mood to relent. It dispersed only after an assurance was given by the Dean and the staff present that he would be expelled forthwith. There were victory cries all over as if a war was won.

So the following day, the offender was sent home, much to the delight of certain students. No one cared about the career, family and social embarrassment of the unfortunate soul. It is a different matter that the same protesters may now be defending their own offsprings indulging in such acts.

I still recall his face while walking down the stretch from the hostel to the staff quarters – head held high, eyes fixed at the horizon – an impassive face, bereft of emotion – just like the French aristocrats walking towards the guillotine during the Revolution.

Times have changed as have our perceptions and attitudes. Colonial and Draconian acts need to be reviewed prudently and amended or scrapped, as deemed proper by the lawmakers.

Mentally Yours

We Indians are too fond of forums, associations, federations, clubs etc. Primarily, to boost ourselves up. We form them at the drop of a hat, and at the slightest hint of 'getting' a plum post. Dwarka is no exception. In fact, it has a high ratio of forums and federations vis-'a-vis the population. It has federations within federations; Each one vying for the limelight. Disgruntled by just a few differences of opinion in a particular forum, the angry members quickly constitute a separate forum. This is easy because there are no regulations or restrictions. Just have a meeting at the aspiring President or Secretary's place over hot pakoras or samosas and steaming tea, blast the committee you just had a brush with, get hold of some willing and unwilling patrons and accord a mouthful name to the new forum. And, lo and behold, there you are. Descended upon the social scene.

I, too, had many chances to be in forums, federations, samities, associations. With my Devil's Advocate reputation and vacillating mind, I did not last long in any of these in any capacity except as a member. I was a member just for the sake of it. However, I still get invitations to join such organisations. I do attend some formation meetings where biscuits and namkeens do the rounds and cheap marigold garlands are thrust down the necks of obliging patrons, DDA and MCD officials, law keepers and the like, with a roving photographer in tow, clicking away from all conceivable angles while the power holder (the man at the centre of this show) of the forum extols the good works and promises of the garlanded ones.

My brush with the forums has made me realise that every organisation has the following categories of persons whose percentage presence makes and defines the organisation. I would like to share my thoughts on this with my readers who may agree or disagree with me, or, who may like to add on:

Fundamental—This category comprises persons who float the organisation either with social motives or personal motives. They dictate the proceedings, make the rules, bend the rules and cling to power until the very end. The motives of this category make or break the organisation.

Ornamental—This category is inducted for face value. The people who belong to it either have a pleasing and imposing personality or some sort of social standing. They hardly perspire or conspire. All they do is silently sign the proceedings without having a look at them. They are a harmless lot and they are better left alone. They occupy visible seating positions where they sit through like zombies as if listening to a philosophical lecture and then suddenly intensely looking at the wrist watch, and leaving the meetings in a hurry.

Sentimental—This category is very difficult to contain. Its members are highly emotional and tend to take umbrage at even innocuous utterings. They are to be handled with kid gloves and though they try to sit in the front, they can be effectively neutralised by sandwiching them between fundamentals. They dislike being disrupted during their submissions and leave the venue in a huff when hurt, which happens quite often. It is easy to calm them down as they are not vindictive or scheming.

Detrimental—The most dangerous category in any organisation is this one. These gents and ladies have a fixed smile or smirk on their faces and nod effusively during discussions while planning moves for a coup d'etat. They are the hyenas of the organisation, moving in packs or alone for a kill. They poach on dissenting members or sentimental ones, counsel them for revolt and assure them support, which never comes at the required moment. Their percentage determines the life of any organisation – which is short, if they outnumber – and long, if they are outnumbered.

Mental—All other members fall under this category, like me, for they become a part of this charade named FORUM.

Now dear readers, close your eyes, think seriously for a few moments and fit yourself and your friends into one of these categories. Which one do you belong to?

The Mullingar Hotel

Holidays are around the corner. Newspapers are full of enticing vacation deals. Full of promises for an exciting, economical, fun filled time. All inclusive deals with different plans and tariffs. The net savvy gang browses through hotels on the Internet. One can have a virtual tour of the place one chooses to stay in, and get the best discounts, too. It is altogether a different story that the actual place may be a pale shade of what is depicted on the Net. During our salad days, we did not have this choice. Bags in hand, families left for the railway platform or the bus stop. Looking for hotels came later. Of course, weekend tourism was not in.

It was mostly during the summer vacations that people travelled. While studying at the Roorkee University in 1973, during our summer training at Dehradun, a group of three, including me, planned to spend a weekend in Mussourie. So, off we went, on a State transport bus to the Queen of the hills, thirty-five kms away from Dehradun. The summer rush had begun. We wandered around to get a room suited to our meagre budget. We looked for hours. Tired, and without success, we sat down at a tea stall near the main bazaar, sipping a sugary syrup called tea and discussing our next move. A haggard looking Gurkha youth sat opposite us, all the while gobbling up what we said, and smiling through his eyes. 'Room mangta? Sasta?', he butted in, uninvited. 'Bohuut bada hotel, bada bada room, twenty-four ghanta nal ka pani, atecch bathroom, garam khana aur sasta. Aapke matlaab ka,' he offered. Our legs were numb as was our mind. The search operations had taken their toll on us. Therefore, his words were like the sound of music to us at that point. We nodded in unison, and having paid the tea stall owner, set forth after him with our kitbags over our shoulders. We did not notice the grin on the stall owner's face. The youth took a steep hill track and we followed him. The track meandered through tall pine trees, getting denser as we walked along. The sun was setting down, the Gurkha kept walking at a brisk pace, humming a gurkhali song and sometimes egging us to keep up pace. 'Kahan hai bhai tumhara hotel?,' I nearly screamed, exasperated. 'Bas, aa giya,' he replied.

By now, we could see Mussourie down below from the hill top we had climbed for about twenty minutes or so. Shortly, the smiling Gurkha turned to us and pointed down to the other side of the hill with a gracious bow. We scrambled to the top to see the hotel and stood stupefied. About five hundred meters down the vallley, stood a once majestic bungalow, L-shaped, with a big compound. Hundreds of Tibetan prayer flags fluttered in the breeze, and dogs and children lazed around. The building was crumbling, half of the roof tiles were missing, and it wore a haunted look. We looked at each other and knew that there was no chance of withdrawing, at that hour. Resigned, we followed the guide, who took us to the hotel compound, and picking up few stones, drove away the dogs, and led us into a big hall. It was then that we saw the board 'MULLINGAR HOTEL. Estd.1887'. About eighty-five years of existence. By now, darkness had descended upon us, and someone had switched on the lights – dim and yellowish. The guide ushered in an old man – apparently the manager – who spread out a big register for filling details. Too tired to look at the room, we settled on an amount of Rs12 per person for a night, and picking up our bags, once again followed the gurkha through a crumbling corridor with abrupt turns to the rear of the massive edifice to an area opening out to a courtyard offering a breathtaking view of a well lit valley. 'Landour Valley, sahib,' the Gurkha said, as if he knew what we were thinking of.

The room door creaked as if in protest. It was a large room – the size of a quarter of a football field. The roof was very high with a wooden, false ceiling hanging precariously. There was a putrid smell and the beds were cold. There was no attached toilet. So, I asked, 'bhai, attached bathroom kahan hai?' He beckoned me out and pointed towards a toilet. 'Arey, yeh to bahar hai. Attach kahan hai?' To which, his nonchalant response was, 'Aapke room ke deewar se attach hai ki nahi?'. Upset, I went in. It was a huge toilet with a broken Indian seat. A bucket full of water was under a brass tap. I opened the tap. Only air came out of it. 'Kya bhai, tum to kah rahe tthey chaubees ghantey paani aata hai?' He retorted, 'Sahab, Landour mein paani aayega, tabhi toh iddhar aayega.' He grinned sheepishly. 'Chalo, hum aapko ek balti paani aur bhejta,' he said. Mighty generous? He vanished from the scene, leaving the three idiots staring at each other. Half an hour passed. Another person came in with half a bucket of water, and informed us in a resigned tone that this was 'fortunately' the last stock. He made clear that the next supply would come only the next day at noon. He also brought in three blankets which had numerous holes and only offered psychological solace. 'Khane mein kya lenge saab?' he asked, raising hopes of a hearty meal. 'Kya kya milega?' my friend enquired. 'Rice aur mutton curry, saab,' was the response.

'Thik hai. Teen plate. Jaldi le aao. 8.30 tak. bhookh lagi hai,' we told him. Time passed eternally. We dozed off – too tired to wait for dinner, which finally arrived at 10.30. The plates were broken on the edges. The grand floral designs on them had withered with time. The rice was cold, and we found to our dismay that there were no mutton chunks in the curry. The bearer had by then slunked off, never to return. Hungry to the core, we lapped up the dinner and retired to our beds. Though it was summer, a cold breeze wafted through the big windows of the room, and the eerie silence all around was broken often by flying owls, screeching monkeys and the piercing, low tone laughter of hyenas. I tried to sleep but images of injured soldiers, huddled and pining to go back to England, haunted me. We dressed up early morning and woke up the old manager. The dinner experience stopped us from asking for tea. While paying, we enquired about the Gurkha and was told that he stayed in the bazaar, and by now, must be scouting for new boarders.

So, we said, 'He assured us that the food would be hot. But there was not even mutton in the curry.' The old man smiled generously, showing off his silver plated teeth, and said, 'Saab, jab banaya tha, garam tha. Jaate jaate thanda ho gaya. Aur aapko mutton ka curry bola to curry diya. Mutton ka baat to nahi kiya. Hafte bhar pehle bana saab, mutton kaise bachega.' The meaning of that sentence hit us when we came out of that hall. We nearly vommitted. While going back in the afternoon, we saw that Gurkha – smiling to the breadth of his face at us. I felt like running down and beating him up but ended up smiling back at him. At least he got us a bed.

P.S.: Mullingar Estate was set up in 1825 by Captain Young, who discovered Mussourie, and the estate served as a settling place for English soldiers later. Turned into a hotel, it fell into disuse in 1947, and now houses Tibetan refugees. On moonlit nights, Captain Young rides in on horseback, visiting his place of love – as the folklore goes.)Times have changed. But the smooth talking and the fake offers still remain. Only the haggard looking Gurkha has been replaced by erudite hotel agents in suits and ties. Happy vacations to all of You!

The Bandhan

Raksha Bandhan is around the corner. Essentially a Hindu festival, it means 'bond of protection'. Observed on the full moon day of Shravana, it is celebrated in many parts of India and Nepal. Typically, on this day, brothers and sisters get together, sisters tie Rakhi on the wrists of brothers, perform aarti, apply tilak. The brother promises to protect the sister and gives her a gift. She offers him sweetmeats. The festival celebrates the love and the duty between siblings. However, it is also used to celebrate any brother-sister relationship though they may not be biologically related. The history of this festival dates back thousands of years. It is said that in 326 BC, when Alexander the Great invaded India, his wife sent a sacred thread to Porus, the Hindu king, with a request not to harm her husband in battle. Legend says that in the battle, even though Porus had many chances, he did not attack Alexander personally.

Another historical example is that of Rani Karnavati of Chittor and Mughal emperor Humayun. She sent the rakhi to Humayun to fend off the impending attack from the Sultan of Gujarat – Bahadur Shah. Humayun set off immediately but was a tad late. Chittor had already fallen to Bahadur Shah. In the eighteenth century, Sikh Khalsa armies tied rakhis on the farmers as a promise to protect them from Muslim armies. In 1849, after the fall of the Sikh empire, the wife of Maharaja Ranjit Singh, Maharani Jindan, was given refuge in Nepal, as the ruler of Nepal had accepted her as his Rakhi sister.

In 1905, the British Empire divided Bengal on the basis of religion. Rabindra Nath Tagore, the Nobel Laureate for literature and a great poet, arranged a ceremony, and got the Hindus and Muslims to tie Rakhis on each other to strengthen the bond of love and unity. Though the division was later reversed and Tagore's appeal was unsuccessful, the festival and his tradition continue in most parts of West Bengal as people tie Rakhis to their neighbours and friends.

Now this was History (His story). I have my story. While we were children, we looked forward to Rakhi. I do not have a biological sister. There were many sisters though – mostly didis in my colony. Meena didi, Lata didi. Sneha didi, Nazma didi, Guddi didi and others. Hindus, Muslims, Sikhs – we lived in a casteless and classless society in the colony. These didis used to tie Rakhis on our wrists and treat us with homemade sweets, namkeens and puri sabji. We did not give any gift back. That was not expected from kids. So, it used to be a bonanza day for us. We paid back the entire year by running errands for these sisters of ours. Getting stationery from the nearby market, getting their clothes from the washerman, and in some cases, delivering love letters.

As we grew up, and our half pants gave way to trousers, moustache lines came out and the world looked colorful, and outlook changed. At that age, every girl seemed like

Sadhana, Nanda, Madhubala, and even a furtive look from them sent our heads spinning and tongues wagging. No one except for our biological ones was a sister for us. Rakhi day became a nightmare for us. Apart from getting into the brother-sister relationship, there was gift in the form of money involved. At least Rs10 per sister.

So, we tried to avoid the 'bond' (in every sense of the term). We were also trying to avoid a relationship which we did not want at that age. Once, on Rakhi, I woke up late. Realising that I had to slink away from home before the aspiring sisters from the neighborhood caught up, I took a quick bath, gobbled down breakfast and dressed up. My elder brother had already ejected out safely, leaving me stranded. I proceeded towards the stairs when I heard giggles and footsteps. The girls were coming, gaily dressed, holding plates containing Rakhis and Akshat, to safeguard themselves from loose cannons like us.

I turned back, avoiding my mother, and like a seasoned athlete, dived under a double bed. The floor was full of dirt, as the maid, as usual, had not swept the area. She probably never did. Two steel trunks lay there, and I curled up, holding my breath. The girls came into the room and looked for me. My mother thought I was still in. Unable to find me, they sat on the bed. My mother called out to me, unsuccessfully, and empathised with the girls. All the while,

I lay breathless, motionless and speechless under that bed. A tiny mouse, coming out from behind the trunks, watched me curiously for some time, and noting that I was not there to interfere in his affairs, retreated to his kingdom. Seconds passed, minutes passed, and the girls made no move to go away. Then, losing all hope of finding me, they finally decided to look for another 'victim', and left. I waited for some time and then came out. I was safe for a year and forty rupees richer.

At this sunset age of my life, I reflect on this episode with amusement, and regret my actions. Paradoxical thought though. Amused at the way I had acted, and regret for having missed out on sisters. HAPPY RAKHI.

The Bisleri Brigade

The Muthoot Hospital plot in Sector 10 has become a hot spot for YOGIs and other religious gurus due to its enormous open space and the proximity to the

Metro Stations. However, the roads around it are reserved for BHOGIs.... As night descends, lovelorn couples, forlorn couples, runaway couples, and amorous couples converge on these roads to enjoy unhindered bliss. Much later, after these couples wrap up their dreams and scamper away to their realities, friends of Bacchus land up, armed with newspaper wrapped bottles full of colored water, and enjoy it, sitting on motorcycles, cars and kerbstones. Broken glass bottles and empty wrappers of namkeen are the grim reminder of the night gone by.

The plot between Muthoot and the upcoming hotel is frequented by TYAGIs – the deadliest lot. Throughout the day, but especially during the mornings and evenings, scores of people frequent this vacant plot with mineral water bottles in hand for Tyaga of a special kind. This blatant open defecation has been going on there for months altogether, but no one has the civic sense or responsibility to put an end to this pollution. This attack on our senses. Though there are a number of societies around, not one has raised any objection to this obnoxious action by the 'BISLERI BRIGADE'. And, Dwarka is supposed to be a 'No Tolerance Zone'. The Labour Welfare department, responsible for checking the facilities provided by builders, is busy with its own welfare. Maybe, this is because we are basically very tolerant people. We tolerate rapes, corruption, snatching, eve-teasing! So, why not defecation? In the open! At least, Dwarka will be more fertile.

Years ago, I had the opportunity to visit one of my friends in Bombay – oops – I am very sorry, no offence meant – Mumbai. He used to stay in a dignified chawl in Dadar. The occupants had a common toilet. When I entered the toilet in the morning, I was fascinated to see assorted tins of Dalda, Rath and Gagan hanging on one wall, with kholi numbers crudely painted on them. I brought down my friend's Rath ka dibba and entered one of the cubicles. I had barely settled down when there was an impatient barrage of knocks, and hurrying on, I cut my finger from the jagged end of the lid rim. The very same day, I shifted to a hotel, to have a safer mode of ablution. I am quite sure that by now those colorful dabbas have been replaced by safer Bisleri bottles. JAI HO BISLERI BRIGADE.

Parkin(G)son's Disease

It's rare to see a scratchless car in Dwarka. Courtesy – high speed driving, teenage drivers, road rage, and to top all that – a painful absence of parking space. While earmarking commercial spaces, the designers did not reckon the traffic volume, present or future. The result is a mad scramble for parking space in markets. The main roads are supposed to be no parking areas, and from time to time, the tow-away cranes do their job gleefully, making one poorer by a few hundred rupees. The space in front of markets is choked with delivery vans, cars belonging to shopkeepers, health club freaks and the like, with hardly any space for shoppers. Getting out of this Mahabharata-style 'Chakravuyha' will seem like child's play, in case you venture to enter the area.

The same is the story of the parking problems faced by residents near schools which have been so thoughtfully (?) allotted space in residential sectors. National, Antinational, International, Global and Local schools park their huge buses all over the road creating severe traffic problems and hazards. My friend had recently purchased a Honda City, and initially took it around proudly to show it off. One sortie near a school resulted in a long scratch along the sleek body and an abrupt end to his flaunting spree. A few days ago, I took my guests from Chandigarh, who were short on time, to a guided tour of our Sector 6 market. It was, unfortunately, a Saturday, and it was about 8pm. I had to hover around the roads like a grounded vulture for about half an hour to find a slot, gap, and gully – whatever you may call it. Finally, my luck seemed to favour me. Not one, but two cars at one time, slunk off. Delighted, I slid my vehicle in and started to prepare for descent. As the left side did not have any space to alight, we had to get down from the right. Suddenly a car swerved in into the right vacant space, leaving hardly any space for us to disembark. A lady, mobile clung to her ear, alighted, and before I could protest, vanished into the crowd. We were stuck. Stuck like a cucumber in a sandwich. I could not even reverse because of the closeness of the two slices squeezing us. I tried to squeeze myself out by adapting all the Yoga asanas I had learnt, tried Baba Ramdev's techniques.

But it was just not my day. My ever-increasing tummy betrayed me. So, we sat in the stuck car, discussed civic problems, politics, personal problems and everything under the sun, all the while craning our necks to look for the lady. At last, she came, packets in hand, mobile precariously stuck between shoulders and ear, and without even bothering to look aside at her hapless victims, reversed and zoomed off. Our market darshan was over. The ladies were glum, the children were upset, and I felt guilty. Guilty of having spinelessly accepted the shortcomings that can still be rectified by raising unified voices of concern, guilty of having surrendered to unlawful actions, deviations, encroachments, violations, and acting as dormant citizens.

However, now the very thought of driving down to the market makes me shudder, my limbs tremble, and I feel like a sack of potatoes. Do they call it 'PARKINGSON'S DISEASE' in medical parlance? Indeed, they must!

To Hell - with Love

Some years ago, I was recuperating after a byepass surgery at Batra Hospital. As usual, I dreamt. Normally, while dreaming, I hang around in

California, Singapore, at the Swiss Alps and in other exotic locations. I do not hang around alone. My companions are Pamela Anderson, Shakira, and Paris Hilton, among others. I do not take my family along on such trips. I cannot hang around these places when I am awake. But that night, I went to Hell. All alone. Two burly Yamadoots with curly hair ushered me into a big hall. It reminded me of Ramanand Sagar's set. At the centre, Lord Yama – the God of death, sat on a throne. An old man sat immersed in a big, ledger sort of book. I presumed that he was Chitragupta – the record keeper. Yama's official carrier, the Buffalo, was near the throne, ruminating; it had a smirk on its face. It was looking straight at me. The face seemed familiar. Lord Yama was busy watching 'Saas Bhi Kabhi Bahu Thi' on a black and white TV. (Colour not allowed in hell.) He didn't have time for an ordinary mortal. I looked hard at the buffalo's face, and I remembered. He was the Blueline bus driver, who often overtook me on the busy Dwarka flyover during office hours. He used to look at me with a smirk that reminded me of the one on Laloo Prasad Yadav's face, as he spoke of the CBI, and asked – 'kya kar lega?' Later, as per the Blueline manual, this driver ran over some unfortunate commuters, and was beaten to death by bystanders.

By now the serial was over. Lord Yama sighed, yawned, looked around, and then, with a resigned but resounding voice, enquired about me. I stood with folded hands. Chitragupta started blurting out my curriculam vitae – good deeds and bad ones. For the sake of secrecy, I will not share the list of my deeds with my dear readers. But, Yama looked pretty bemused. After a pause, he asked me, 'So, you are from Dwarka? Our Krishna's place, eh? Gopies all around? Must be a heavenly place to live in?'

'No, no, Sir,' I protested vehemently. 'It's not Krishna's Dwarka. It is the DDA's Dwarka. A living hell, Sir. No water, no streetlights, no multiplex, no security, no hospital. Only chain snatching, car jacking, promises and taxes,' I said.

'And, you claim to have stayed there for the last five years,' Yama asked, with apparent awe and astonishment. 'Yes, my Lord,' I managed to say. Yama thought about this. Then, he said, 'Well, as you have already served your time in hell, you need not revisit it. You are being sent to heaven for the rest of the term.' I was thrilled. Soon, I was being airlifted by two smiling Apsaras – each one holding my hand. I was yet to decide which one was more beautiful when I was woken up. I faced two stone faced nurses with injections in their hand, waiting to prick me. Smile was a mile away. Yet another day on this earth… had begun.

From the Diary of a Bank Manager

16 November: Woke up at 6am. The day promises to be hectic and tough. Contrary to assurances, the currency chests are bringing only 20% cash

requirement. The queues are getting longer and the wait for money even more so. No off on Saturday and Sunday. Pooja came and literally cried as she was to go outstation for a marriage. Now, she cannot. She has to manage the exchanges. The guard bhaiyya – an old ex-army man is tired and drained. God knows how to handle the situation. Never studied about this sort of crisis management in management school.

17 Nov: I am a second-generation banker. My father rose from the ranks to become a manager in a Nationalised bank in the late seventies. While he faced 'Nasbandi' – the sterilisation wave, I am facing 'Notebandi' – the Demonetisation wave. About forty years later.

Nasbandi was meant to control the menace of population. Notebandi is ostensibly to control the menace of Black money. However, after forty years of the diktat, we have a mammoth population of about a hundred and twenty crores. So, to what extent Notebandi helps is a thing to look forward to. Would it go the Nasbandi way?

21 Nov: All of a sudden, I am the most sought after person in the neighbourhood. Everyone is snuggling up to me. The Hi-hello conversation always turn to – 'Naye note mil jayenge?' How do I tell them that I have Rs6,000 given by my father in my right pocket,Rs8,000 given by my brother-in-law in my left pocket, and Rs6,000 in my

shirt pocket, all waiting to be changed? Some enterprising managers have turned this scarcity of notes into a profitable venture in connivance with their regular and trusted customers. I have sympathies for them. I am also getting feelers from prime customers to help them out or face exodus when normalcy returns. So what do I do? Follow my conscience and lose business? Or???????

We Indians may be uneducated, underfed and impoverished but when it comes to ingenuity, we beat all others hollow. Within hours of withdrawl of the notes, people thronged to buy Gold, buy Dollars, buy Flight and First-class train tickets; they devised all conceivable ways to convert the money. The change was swift.

22 Nov: People ask why there was no prior intimation of this step. That reminds me of a story I read. There was a fire in a godown filled with potatoes. People passing by feasted on the burnt potatoes. One of them went across to the godown next door and asked the owner, 'Sir, when is your godown getting burnt? I will bring along some salt to go with the potatoes. Missed the taste this time.' Well, disasters never come with prior notice. No money for the last two days. An aged customer waited in vain for the money standing in a queue for two consecutive days. I saw his drawn-out face pressed against the steel grill door for hours. Does he look like a black money hoarder? Why are

they suffering for no fault of theirs? All these days never saw the high and mighty customers having to queue up. Wonder why? The intent of demonetization may be noble, but the implementation is questionable. But then, who would say that the King is naked? Not even the kid on the street. The tailors have spun an imaginary yarn around the King and vanished.

2 Dec: Nearly half the promised fifty days of this hassle is over. Still, no relief is in sight. One is fed up the 'NO CASH' board. It isn't easy to explain constraints to customers. Tempers are running high. The initial show of patience is giving way to frustration and anger.

The condition of the bank staff is like that of unfortunate Indian soldiers armed with old 303 rifles but short of bullets to face the Chinese troops during the 1962 war. But they bear it stoically, hoping that the future – one without black money, will dawn upon them. Hope is a good dope for the gullible masses.

Cry my beloved country!

(No more entries found).

The Ventilator

Yamraja was pacing frantically in the corridor. He looked tense. He held a page in his hand and glanced at it from time to time. He had called Chitragupta, his record keeper, and was waiting for him to arrive. His celestial carrier, the Buffalo, was sitting nearby, eyes half closed and cud coming out from his mouth. He bellowed when he saw Chitragupta sauntering in, which made Yamraja turn and accost him. 'Dev,' said Chitragupta, bowing in reverence, What made you call this servant of yours in such haste?' 'Chitragupta, what is going on?' asked Yamraja. 'All the arrivals are late as per the list. Look here, last week, five out of ten people, supposed to reach here on Monday, did not turn up. It is the same, this week, too. What is stopping them from coming when I have already signed their death warrants?'

Fixing his gaze on the floor, Chitragupta replied, 'Dev, a group of people in Prithvilok is delaying the release of bodies. Consequently, those souls are stuck in the immigration bay. We do not allow entry until the body is burnt or buried.'

Yamraja:	Who are these audacious people?
Chitragupta:	Nursing homes, Dev. They keep the bodies under a machine called the ventilator until....
Yamraja:	Until what?
Chitragupta:	Until the mediclaim limit is exhausted or the FDs are completely used up.
Yamraja:	What! Who gave them that right?

Chitragupta: The insurance companies and the nursing home management. Of course, sometimes, when a richer patient comes, the poorest patient occupying the bed is officially declared dead and released.

Yamraja: Strange! Never knew of this. I would like to see the episodes directly.

Chitragupta: Dev, you have cataract. You may not be able to see. Should I call Sanjay?

Yamraja: Sanjay? He of the Mahabharata? Ok. Call him! (Chitragupta sends word through a sentry, and Sanjay is brought in.)

Chitragupta: Sanjayji, how are you doing?

Sanjay: Oh, fine, Guptsree. It is fun here without Duryodhana and his ruffians.

Chitragupta: Dev wants you to use your divine sight and tell him what is going on in one of the nursing homes in the Prithvilok Capital, New Delhi.

Sanjay: Ah, my Hastinapur? How I'd love to see it again.

Yamraja: (impatiently) Quick! I have other things to do. (Sanjay trains his eyes, and after adjustments, speaks out.)

Sanjay: Dev! *Adharma Khestre Hastinapur Rugnalaya Maddhye*—(Yamraja cuts him short).

Yamraja: Stop! Stop! Do not use that obsolete language.

No one knows that now. Speak in a language that we can understand.

Sanjay: Well, Dev, I see a lobby with plush interiors, Italian sofas, vertical A/Cs, air purifiers, and a grand reception with beautiful girls manning it.

Yamraja: Are you describing a hospital or a hotel?

Chitragupta: They are all the same, Dev. Package system. Seven days and nights, ten days, eleven nights. You name it.

Sanjay: Dev, they are bringing in an old man of about eighty-five, on a stretcher. He is complaining of stomach pain. Two doctors arrive, check the abdomen, and are now discussing amongst themselves. Now, one well-dressed gentleman accosts the son of the patient. He is asking whether the patient has medical reimbursement. The son replies in the affirmative. A broad smile can be seen on the face of a staff member. He conveys that to the doctors. They spring into motion, and are now discussing. (He strains his ears.)

Yamraja: Try listening to what they say.

Sanjay: The senior one is saying that it is just a case of flatulence. But they may prolong the test process for a week or ten days. The junior one asks about 'what' to diagnose. The senior takes out a pen and writes 'Factotum Aneurysm Rectumistis Turbulence'.

Yamraja: By Rambha, what a disease!

Chitragupta: Dev, Read the first words! It is FART. Simply obstructed gas, given a high-sounding name.

Yamraja: They could have just given him some ajwain powder with hot water. I take it, myself.'

Chitragupta: Dev, In that case, how will these men get hold of the Mediclaim money?

Yamraja: (agitated) This is highly unethical. Call the Ashwini Brothers! They must take action. And, give me the names of the hospital staff. I will issue warrants.

Chitragupta: No! No! Dev, Never do that!

Yamraja: Why?

Chitragupta: They might just open up a nursing home here. And, put you on the ventilator.

Bai, Bahu and Bayu

Of late, I have started going to the neighbourhood park in the mornings. To walk and to breathe air like numerous other health aficionados. I realise that I have missed out on a lot. As there was a big board prohibiting, inter alia, the entry of dogs, I couldn't venture in. Pardon, I mean I had a dog, after all.

Now, my pet having passed away, I can enter freely. Epiphany! I am miffed to note that there are more than a dozen strays pooping and urinating on the grass over which the walkers so solemnly tread and exercise. Gau matas also find their way to the frolic at times. And then, there are the *Aswachacha* people spewing phlegm with utter casualness all over the grass. Anyway, the parks offer great visual and listening pleasure, especially if one has the caliber of studying human nature. Watch the walkers. The study could enlighten you to the motley crew flailing their limbs along with their quirks. Some prefer walking clockwise, some anti-clockwise; all duly based on the *gyaan* they receive from TV channels. Some walk with long strides, some short ones. Some perform breaststrokes in the air, while some walk with flaccid limbs. In a short span, I have come to apprehend my own set of morning walkers. Allow me to share.

The first one is the 'Lone Ranger' type. They walk alone, lost in themselves, and often sighted with earphones plugged in – ostensibly to dissuade others from getting into a conversation. They walk with their glass bead eyes lowered at a brisk pace, ignoring even their known ones, lest the walk is interrupted. The second type is of 'Couple Walkers'. This type generally consists of couples walking in tandem; one of them doing the talking and the other listening without once breaking the rhythm. The conversation ranges from the wayward son, arrogant daughter-in-law, property grabbing relatives and topics which they cannot comfortably discuss back home.

The third type is 'Group Walkers'. This consists of four or five like-minded ones, who discuss and decide the country's present and future, while circling the park. From the weather to 'Poletix'. From Advaniji's future to Trump's policy. To sidestep them is a tough task.

The last type is the 'Reluctant walker'. This variety is generally averse to walks, and has been prodded out of bed by concerned (or sadistic) better halves, kids or doctors. So, they walk limpidly, grabbing any chance offered to shake hands, and to get an unsuspecting listener to hear their story of the day. Then, seemingly exhausted by the verbal walk, they slump onto the nearest bench.

The most interesting spots in the parks are the benches. Here, the neighbourhood uncles and aunties discuss, complain and comfort each other about three important things of their sunset years. *BAHU* (daughter-in-law), *BAI* (maid) and *BAYU* (gas). One has to just slink in with an impassive face into the available space on the bench and eavesdrop. The *Saas-Bahu* topic is evergreen and perdurable. As no Bahus are in the vicinity, the outpourings of vitriol against them goes on, unabated. I am fairly sure that writers of the Saas-Bahu serial genre gorge and churn out stories slyly occupying these benches. The other day, I heard an old lady saying, 'bahu khud to ek maxi mein din bhar leti rahti hai aur TV dekhti hai, aur mujhe kehti hai ki roj sabere saj dhaj ke park jaati hain – chakkar kya hai? Bolo koi baat hui?', drawing sympathetic nods from the listeners. Prompted, this sort of bashing continues. Bais are next on the list, and their growing demands and sudden absence is a favorite topic. The last subject – of Vayu is better not delved into here. It spoils the day (and night) – inevitable but obnoxious.

I walk out of the park, lungs filled with fresh air, and mind full of with stale talk. I thank the TV gurus for at least waking people up from their slumber, and for seeking ways to mitigate life's woes. Opinions differ about the ways of keeping good health, but the aim remains the same. As I come out, I hear anguished laughter, resembling a hyena's howl, from the park. A group is trying Yoga. More on that later. Getting late for the morning tea.

The Sixth Mughal

They have done it. The 'ALAMGIR' – the sixth Mughal emperor of the Mughal dynasty has been stripped of his place, in the city of his coronation and subsequent rule of forty-nine long years. In a hurried midnight operation, to avoid possible backlash, the NDMC renamed Aurangzeb Road as Dr APJ Abdul Kalam Road. There was no backlash though. For the new name was that of Independent India's most loved President (arguably) and a great scientist. And, the name he replaced was that (as we have been fed for ages) of an intolerant bigot. Sporadic murmurs, however, continue to emerge in the form of blogs, articles and editorials.

In fact, to me, Aurangzeb was a better emperor than Humayun, Jahangir and ShahJahan, and was nearly equal to Akbar, as he expanded the empire to enviable limits. He, by his ruthless ambitions, achieved what his predecessors could not. His yearly tributes were unmatched by anyone in the world. He subdued the mighty Rajputs, who could rebel only after his death at the age of eighty-eight. He opined that the royal treasury was held in trust for the citizens of the Empire. He copied the Holy Quran and stitched caps to earn his living.

He has been vastly debased by western historians of the time as he did not pamper them, and he had scant regard for the countries they came from. He brought down officials of the East India Company to their knees from time to time and restrained them. He also prevented the Portugese, the Dutch and the French from entrenching themselves in

India. However, all his attributes were overshadowed by his religious intolerance, revengeful and merciless attitude to his dissenters and the imposition of extra taxes on non-Muslims. This, despite the fact that by all accounts, he donated money to renovate the Mahakal temple at Ujjain, the Prayag Shiv temple in Allahabad and the Umananda temple in Guwahati. It is true that he did not allow new temples to come up. This could have been to contain the spread of other religions.

He was the last of the Great Mughals. No ruler after him could sustain the Empire like he did. Thirteen emperors occupied the throne after him but only the last Mughal – Bahadur Shah Zafar – finds popular mention, not for his attributes but for the Sepoy mutineers who catapulted him to fame in the midst of a tragic end to the Great Empire. But the fact remains that Aurangzeb is a very important part of Indian History, and to obliterate him would be a sad chapter in it.

I am fascinated by the similarities of these two personalities. The name, the positions they held and the passion they had.

While Aurangzeb's full name was 'Abul Mujaffar Muhi-Uddin Mohammad Aurangzeb', Dr Kalam's full name was 'Avul Pakir Jainulabdeen Abdul Kalam'. They were Heads of the Empire and the Nation respectively. They strove to strengthen the Empire and the nation respectively. The similarities end here. While Aurangzeb was by all accounts intolerant of other religions, cruel and manipulative, and abhorred by his subjects, Dr Kalam was the most loved President till date. He ignited fire in minds to achieve the impossible, he was an inspiration, and a compassionate humble man. He deserved a much better tribute than being consigned to an arterial road just to initiate the process of rewriting Indian History.

The British, while naming roads kept out religious, regional and sentimental biases, and gave place to nearly all who shaped India and particularly Delhi. Therefore, even zealots and merciless kings such as Lodi and Tughlaq also found a place in Lutyen's Delhi. If renaming was to be done, there were many roads open for change. Why was Pandara Road not considered? The Raj is long gone. Why then must we have a Rajpath? There is Nyaya Marg, Satya Marg, Niti Marg and Vinay Marg in Chanakyapuri. Delhi is bereft of these attributes. So, why not change them? Just what is Africa Avenue doing bang in the middle? Several important stretches are named after obscure foreign leaders who have lost their relevance even in their own countries.

Dwarka is getting a new diplomatic enclave. There will be a number of roads waiting to be named. Shift the foreign leaders here and rename the roads being occupied by them. Let us rise above religion, beliefs and leanings. Let us stop obfuscating the memories of the emperors, kings and statesmen who ruled or served Delhi and consequently the country. Let evil be present with goodness. To remind us of the fallouts. After all, that is the purpose of History. Let not History become His Story.

Black is Beautiful

I have often wondered why the colour black is associated with something bad or evil. Black magic, black heart, black spot, black money etc. It is such a bold and standout colour. We are obsessed with fairness. For no reason. We hold fairness in awe. That is why the British ruled us for over two centuries. Even now, we refer to a fair person with wide eyes. 'Gora Chitta sa' (Fair) and to a dark person as 'Kala kaluta sa', contorting our faces. But the world's best sportsmen, boxers, cricketers, actors, singers are black. It is time the mindset changed. Black is the colour which defines other colours. As I write, I am reminded of an incident from my childhood.

I was about four or five. A family friend was visiting us. There was a fair girl, about my age. So, we began to play together. And then, as usual, we picked up a fight. She said, 'I am not going to play with you. You are Kaala.' It hurt. So, I pushed the girl and she banged her head against a chair, developing a lump on her forehead. All hell broke loose. She cried incessantly, and her parents, with sullen faces, left our place. My parents were very upset. On that day, for the first and last time, I got spanked by my father, an otherwise very cool person. I went on crying, crouched under the dining table, and muttered 'Ami kaala na, Ami sada' (I am not black. I am white.) for a long time. The incident, even after about sixty years, remains etched in my mind. However, I did not learn my lesson, and soon, at the tender age of twelve, fell for a very fair Anglo-Indian girl, my neighbour in our railway colony in Lucknow. That was the first of my numerous one-sided loves. Her name was Glenda Michael Townsend Booth. I often acted like Tom Sawyer, standing precariously on the common boundary wall, singing and dancing, much to the delight of my fair lady and her cousins. I was on cloud nine. Once, I gave her a couple of baby rabbits out of my large rabbit family. One morning, I heard her panic shouting, 'Subir! – Subir!' and like a Holy Knight, ran out, clutching my striped Pajant (a cross between a pajama and a pair of pants), and faced her. Tears were streaming down her plump red cheeks and she said, 'A mongoose has taken away my rabbits.'

This was a new word for me, with my very limited UP wallah English. So, excusing myself, I ran back to my study table, opened the Bhargava's English to Hindi dictionary and looked for 'mongoose'. There it was – Newla – in Hindi. Knowing the culprit, I went back to Glenda and consoled her. 'See, Glenda, a mongoose would not take two rabbits at one go. They must be around here in the bushes.' Then gathering together my ever-obliging friends, I searched the lawn, oblivious of thorny scratches, and fished out the furry delights from a drain where they had wandered off. The profuse thanking from the fair lady changed my gait for a few days and I felt like Detective Rip Kirby, a famous cartoon strip character of those days. I also started putting in more time to read English and tried to initiate conversation while she came back from school through the colony lanes. I got emboldened when her cousin Maria fell for a tall, dark, handsome railway engineer, Krishnan, and eventually married him. But I am neither tall nor handsome; just dark. So, I stood just about a 33% chance of making it. Still, the Dark Knight did not lose heart. My campaign was cut short with my father's transfer to Kanpur.

As long as Krishnans get married to Marias, I am happy. For, it is not the exterior colour that matters. It is the colour of the heart that does. Hearts, fortunately, are of the same colour.

The Third Clap

This anecdote relates to one of the numerous cousins of my father. An exodus from erstwhile East Bengal in 1945-46 saw most able-bodied people from my father's native village in Khorsedpur (Selaidah) joining East Indian Railways in various capacities. Dhanbad was the main center. This uncle of mine joined the coal movement department. He was fastidious about food. He lived to eat. He was not a voracious eater, but he was discerning. He remained a bachelor and unfortunately died of cancer. He wore an immaculately clean white dhoti with a half shirt over it – with sprays of snuff: his brush with addiction. To supplement his meagre salary, he worked as payment recovery agent on a part time basis.

For realising the payments, he had to visit Calcutta often – to the gaddis of Marwari coal merchants in the Barabazar area. The gaddis were in serpentine byelanes, often enough only for two persons to cross. Dirty nullahs ran along the lanes and the Gaddis were run from dingy rooms containing a low wooden Takthposh, a cotton mattress covered with white sheets, an assortment of pillows. A fan used to wearily go on, fed through DC supply – never allowing it to reach peak speed. The rooms were lit with low watt bulbs. The walls had half the gods from the Indian pantheon adorning them.

One humid afternoon, my uncle went to a seth's gaddi to realise some dues. Two hefty guys sat on stools outside the room, occupying half of the lane's width. The seth was reclining on a bolster, eyes half shut, after lunch. He was massive. He lay there like a white hippopotamus enjoying the afternoon sun on the banks of the Nile. Pleasantries over, the seth made some calculations and gestured to a person crosslegged in a dark corner in front of a wooden desk. He wore thick glasses, and a half kurta, and was an emaciated figure, in stark contrast to the merchant. The seth clapped once. After a while, one of the people sitting outside brought an earthen kullad of hot tea. Barabazar was famous for tea, kachories, lassi, rabri and other food items.

Uncle sipped longingly from the kullad, enjoying the earthy smell. The fan above circled grudgingly, making a sad screeching sound. The gods on the countless calenders on the walls swayed to and fro from the air thrown by the fan, their movement adding to its monotonous sound. The man in the corner counted some money and handed it over to uncle. Now, the seth clapped twice. The man outside the door re-appeared bringing in two hot kachories on a leaf plate. The taste was heavenly. My uncle munched the pieces with the finesse of a connoisseur and wiped his mouth. The seth looked uncomfortable. His torso seemed to squirm. He then apologetically told my uncle that although he loved street food as well, health issues such as acidity did not allow him to indulge. But he loved watching others enjoy themselves. At this point, the seth clapped again thrice. My uncle was ectastic. He could imagine rabri coming now. It was simple, he thought. One clap – tea. Two claps – kachories. Three claps – rabri. He waited in pregnant anticipation. Presently, both the robust guys came in – lifted one of the Roman pillar-like legs of the seth on their shoulders. The seth contorted his face and let out a blast of air. The entire room appeared to shake. The fan seemed to fall silent and the calenders stopped swaying.

Now, my uncle understood the third clap.

He rose and scrambled out, throwing unintelligible pleasantries. Thereafter, he stood bewildered in the lane. He felt like throwing up, and did so in the nullah, stood up, and took fresh air into his lungs. He then walked as fast as he could, vowing never to come back. He felt sorry for the hapless gods.

Moral – expectations and reality are generally opposite to each other.

Being Indradev

A couple of months ago, I came across a news item. An elderly person from a posh locality was held on various charges including impersonation. He posed as a neta and hoodwinked many. The news itself was common – the name was not. It belonged to one of my childhood friends with whom I had played marbles and gilli-danda in Lucknow. The last time we met, it had been in a friend's office where he handed me a card that said that he was the liaision man for more than a dozen companies. Another power broker of Delhi's underbelly, I thought. I deliberately lost that card. Impersonating is not much of an offence depending on the circumstances but he indulged in the flesh trade business as well according to the news item. Not that I am supporting impersonation, but the intent makes the offence vary in severity. God Indra impersonated Sage Gautama and seduced Ahalya. Both were cursed. A case of erotic intent. People impersonated Hitler with an intent to save his life and so on. There are many instances when wittingly or unwittingly, you impersonate. For entertainment, survival or fraud. I would like to share with my readers a story or two when I unwittingly had to impersonate.

It was the early nineties. I was looking after the construction of some flats meant for the CBI staff. It was end December and I was asked by my company to rush to Lawrence School, Sanawar for some work. So, I took my family, too, to spend the New Year in Shimla, not far from Sanawar. I forgot that during that period, it is impossible to get hotel accommodation without prior booking. Still, committed to the family, I took them by train to Shimla. Keeping them in the waiting room, I went out to get a room. It was a futile effort. Then, I remembered that one of the flat owners was posted in the Shimla CBI office. I trudged up to locate the office and the person. However, he was of no help, as all the hotels were full. But he suggested that I should try out the VIP suite at the station and rang up the station master informing him that someone from the office was looking for accomodation and that he could 'please be helped'. So, off I went down the winding lanes of Shimla to the station.

The station master was waiting in his room. After exchanging pleasantaries, he handed me a form to be filled with name and address. All the while he ranted about the risk he was taking by letting out the room meant only for VIPs, just because I was from the CBI. A hot cup of tea had arrived by now and his assistants stood erect nearby. I filled in my name. Then, came the line of reckoning. I had to put the address in a manner that it showed my CBI connection. I racked my brain hard, and then wrote, 'CI, CBI SOC, New Delhi'. I was being another Yudhisthir. CI, CBI SOC meant Construction in-charge, CBI Society. Not an iota of untruth in that. The station master read it as Circle Inspector, CBI, Special Operation Cell. Ashen faced, he, with utmost reverence, led us to the suite, and made us comfortable. Lunch, tea, dinner came in steadily (although I paid for everything) accompanied with dozens of feared salutes whenever we passed through the platform. We stayed there for two days, and I could feel furtive glances from the Maal Gudam, Cafeteria and Ticket checkers. They were all praying for my departure. There were no tickets available for the return journey by the toy train to Kalka. The station master put in all his resources to play to get us the tickets, saw to it that the luggage and the CBI officer were settled, and gave a ramrod namaskar when the train slithered out. I could see the relief on his face and on those of his assistants. Had he noticed my face closely, he would have noticed the same sense of relief on it. I was tenser than him during my stay lest my real identity was revealed and my cover… blown off.

I have one more story to tell you.

In the late nineties, I was overseeing our works at Agartala, its surroundings badly hit by insurgency. We had a retired colonel from the Indian army as our project manager, who was reporting to me. Once, I had to make an unscheduled visit to Agartala. Unfortunately, all the hotels, just a handful of them, were already fully occupied. I had a tiring day and wanted to rest badly. So, Colonel X took me to his former regiment campus to lodge me in one of the

Officers' Guest Houses. As I sat in the car, he went in to meet the commandant and came out beaming. Apparently, he had convinced the commandant to allow me a night over. We pulled up in front of a big bunglow and walked in with a straight gait to be accosted by a JCO manning the mess. Colonel X, in his baritone voice announced, 'I am Col X', and pointing to me, said, 'he is my bass.' Col X, being a pucca Punjabi pronounced boss as 'bass'. The JCO proceeded to verify this from the commandant's office on his phone. I could feel his probing eyes on me. My shoes were full of site dust and my face haggard. But then, I had been a stage actor and an ardent fan of Sir Peter O'Toole.

I have watched the movie 'Night Of The Generals' several times. So, I kept my body straight, head held high, hands behind my back and kept on looking at the shoddy paintings like the General in the movie, avoiding eye contact with the JCO. Thereafter, a batman came, picked my bag, and escorted me to a large suite. 'Kuch lenge, Sahab?' he asked. 'Get me a beer later with some pakoras,' I said, and sunk on the sofa. The batman brought a big register, in which, much to my fear and chagrin, the entry made was – 'Brig SK ADHICARY.' The colonel had announced that I was his boss. So, the JCO had given me the next/ higher rank. That of a Brigadier. I did not go out of the room. I ordered dinner there, and tossed fretfully on the bed for most of the night. The morning brought respite. Colonel Sahab was there early morning and I did not entertain his idea of having breakfast in the mess. I wanted to be out of the mess that I had involuntarily got into. And, I wanted to do that fast.The batman had polished my shoes with into a mirror like surface, and I could see my guilt ridden face on it. The car whizzed out of the campus, and I felt the morning air fill my nostrils. It was freedom from impersonation, after all, even though inadvertent.

Chinese Checkers

Lucknow. 1962. It was a bitter winter. Time for huddling around the anghiti. Then came the news of war. The Sino-Indian war. The crackling radio kept us posted about it and we Indians were fuming with impotent rage over the backstabbing by the Chinese after raising the slogan – 'Hindi-Chini bhai bhai'. The anger got directed towards the small Chinese community in the city. During those days, stone pelting or vicious attacks were not required to frighten people. Taunts and curse words did the job. On the Lalbagh-Kaiserbagh road, there were two shops owned by two Chinese brothers – B Wang and T Wang. One was a dentist, and the other, a shoemaker.

Dental care was the last thing on our minds those days and elite dentists such as Dr Sham Lal were beyond the reach of ordinary denizens. So, for normal dental ailments, the Chinese doctors were preferred. They did not possess any regular degrees but learnt from experience. No questions asked. We used to stop for a while on our way to school to watch families lounging in the sun with passive faces and distant looks dressed in traditional Chinese attire. They were part of our life. The war changed it all. Faced with boycott and jeers, one fine day, they all moved out of town, perhaps to Kolkata, where a sizable Chinese population stayed without trouble, thanks to the communist leanings of the locals there.

The clamour to boycott has risen again. This time, for the dragon having taken the vulture under its wings. And, for helping it overtly and covertly. Boycotting of all

Chinese goods is requested on social media. Shops selling Chinese crackers are being targetted. 'All things Chinese to be avoided,' my friends advise over Whatsapp. So, I muse. I muse over the scenario. I wake up in the morning to the ring of my Chinese clock. I rush to the toilet to open the faucet of Chinese make. I eat Chinese style oats for breakfast. I rush to office and sit on my Chinese made chair and work on a Chinese made table. The coffee maker in the office is Chinese. I call my bearer through a Chinese call bell and he serves me coffee in a (Chinese) Bone China set. I come home, switch on the Chinese LED lights and eat Chinese noodles. Then, I notice with consternation that the bed is imported from China and the bedsheet, too. I strip to sleep with my vest and underwear on, feeling happy that they are Young India banians. I learn later that they are woven on Chinese machines. I am amused that no more Whatsapp and Facebook messages are coming my way. Maybe my friends have realised that they had been using Chinese made mobile phones. I have surmised that to boycott Chinese goods I have to become Amir Khan of PK. But then, the transistor again may be of Chinese origin.

It must be realised that as long as the Chinese have the massive Indian market to do business with, they will play defensive and shall not venture to openly support Pakistan or mount an independent attack. Deprived of the business opportunities, the Dragon may breathe fire – enough to just singe us, not burn us to a cinder.

P.S.: I am no China lover. Its Chairman Mao encouraged revolution in the late sixties, disrupting our studies. Many bright young men, fired by his ideologies, lost their lives, dreaming about a new world. Some of them were my friends. But one has to be pragmatic.

Gifting Times

I love Diwali notwithstanding its high decibel crackers, attendant smog, terrified birds and animals. I simply love it because I am made to feel like a *Maharaja* or an IAS officer for about fifteen days prior to the festival. The callous, dehydrated, emaciated security guards with jaded eyes suddenly spring sprightly, opening gates with youthful vigor and a long salute. The ever-elusive sweeper spends many minutes cleaning my home front until he is acknowledged. A respectful salute again.

The lazy driver exudes gymnast-like attributes with an earlier never-heard-of 'Good morning, Sir' and broad grin on a face which had earlier shown granite like qualities. The office peon is extra helpful. More cups of coffee, tea and biscuits appear frequently. The voice becomes silken. This charade starts about a week or ten days before Diwali and ends on the day I give out, with an artificial smile on my face, '*Diwali ki bakhshish*'. However, the superficial feeling of being treated as a *Bada Sahab* keeps me happy for quite some time. More so, as I stay in Delhi, where a salute does not come for free through the year. I am sure my readers, especially those who stay in Delhi, feel the same.

Diwali is, besides being the festival of lights, a festival of gifts and discounts. The discount reaches an awesome 80%+20% which means one buys the product at just 4% cost. This marketing yoga is a matter of deep research and concern. I will delve into this discount account later. My concern is the way gifting has become synonymous with this auspicious festival. To expect gifts has become a habit, more so of government officials and the staff in power. Attendance remains high in offices before Diwali. No one wants to miss the gifts. Even the most constipated faces are illuminated with expectation.

We, at our PSU, believed in the government circular that 'occasional gifts and parties are allowed – not habitual'. Therefore, there were no qualms about accepting gifts. Station leave requests are also low during this period. Work efficiency, especially in the bill sections, increases manifold, and no one cribs. In some private companies, receiving gifts is not encouraged or is forbidden. The enterprising employees have thought of circumventing this. They hand over their car keys to the person bringing in gifts and ask them to directly keep their gifts in the dickey of their vehicle. The gift is given to the chair, not to the person occupying it. Out of chair. Out of the gift list. The habit of receiving gifts causes immense heart burn to officials, who have just retired, and who find solace in the song – *kaun aayega yahan, koi na aaya hoga/mera darwaja hawaon ne hilaya hoga.*

Selecting gifts for various levels is a process in itself. Distributing them is a project, especially in Delhi and in the NCR. Therefore, thoughtless gifts are distributed in most cases. I have only 10% hair on my hammer head. I received a hair dryer once, much to my chagrin. Factories make a kill. All their rejected stuff gets sold. And these things are sent as recycled gifts. This gifting must be stopped. This puts undue pressure on small businessmen and suppliers. To excel over competitors. To strain finances just to fulfill the formalities.

For 355 days, the dog beats the master to reach the door before the master. For the remaining ten days before Diwali, the master beats the dog to it. *Koi to gift laya hoga*.

The Golo

I wondered why my face looked like an over burnt piece of brown bread. I saw myself in group photographs, where even those with swarthier complexions than mine, managed to glow like LED bulbs. I mustered all the courage I had to ask my wife about it, and as expected, got a mouthful about why I should not attend such social functions, particularly when I did not care much about my attire or the way I looked. From her fifteen minute monologue, I gathered that I must go in for a face clearance exercise or facial, as they say, at a salon before a function.

I should have known. I had been hearing sob stories from my colleagues about their trepidation at getting an invitation to a function. The cost of facials, manicures, pedicures and hair styling was immense. Their wives, daughters or daughters-in-law indulged in these activities; the monthly budget took a hit, and that befuddled them financially. So, they also indulged in getting facial done for themselves as a cost benefit like 'a package for two'.

My mother, my aunts and the other ladies of the house just knotted their long hair neatly into plaits or buns with U clips that, to me, looked like tongs. These helped me pick out ticks from my dog's coat. Clandestinely, of course. They would then dab some Afghan Snow or Himani Snow on their faces, rub it in, and coat it with generous pats of face powder. That was it. Sometimes, the snow was visible in the creases of their neck and glittered.

Gone are those days. A gift to the bride may set you back by Rs2,000 but the preparatory works for such gifting may cost you five to six times that.

So, last week, when I had to attend a marriage, I headed to the nearest and cheapest barber shop, the one I frequent. It is called 'STYLE and GLOW'. The elderly Miyaanji from Bijnore was busy watching Govinda serenading Raveena on an equally elderly television set; reclining on a bench, which was supposed to have customers on it. Being a weekday, the bench and the shop were deserted. 'Aayiey, Janaab, after a long time?' He hauled himself up reluctantly as Govinda drew near Raveena. He knew I was a Rs 100 customer. I had my hair cut just once in six months. Nothing more was expected of me.

He stopped midway while taking out his never sterilised sheet from the cupboard when I enquired about facials. His face brightened in anticipation of a kill, like a leopard spotting a deer. 'Arey, Janaab,' he said. 'I have been asking you each time you've come in whether you would like a facial, as well. But you showed no interest. Do you have to attend an important function, Janaab?' he asked. 'Oh, well, I thought it was long overdue', I muttered incoherently, still unsure about the plunge. 'What sort of facial will you go for? I have a gold package, a silver package, a copper package, a herbal package. Just name it,' he prodded. I sat flabbergasted, wondering how a golden hue would look on my complexion. Or, for that matter, a silver hue. Miyaanji offered to tell me how much they would cost. 'Gold 8000 ka, silver 6000 ka, copper 5000 ka; the herbal package will also cost you nearly the same. Which one would you like?' he asked. 'Oh, no,' I retorted. 'Not so much. I want a cheap one; a really cheap one. Any thing like an earth package – like Multani Mitti sitti?' Miyaanji, like a true barber was an expert at human psychology. He felt that the lamb may turn fugitive any time. Pausing to think a little, he said, 'All right. Let me give you the special 'Style and Golo' facial, only for Rs1,500. Just try it once. Chehere pe golo aa jayegi.' I surmised that 'golo' was 'glow', and nodded concurrence.

Thereafter, there was no escaping from what was in store. Miyaanji had already tied a protective cover around my neck and had pulled up my face. He, then, proceeded to rub, pinch, pull and smear my face with different concoctions, all the while furtively glancing at Raveena. Mask on, I sat like a zombie. The mirror wasn't complimenting me yet. Miyaanji had, by now, set the TV volume low, and putting me into a helpless, no reply position, plunged into Indian politics, the state of cricket, diminishing tolerance et al for about half an hour or so before forcefully lowering my face into a semi dirty basin and cleaning it with an equally dirty towel. I pulled myself up; my face felt a burn, probably from a dose of bleach, and paid Miyaanji what was due to him. My face was not feeling light but my pocket was. I tried to look at my face in the mirror. It did not cooperate. I stepped out into the sunshine, convinced that the brown bread piece had yet to become a malai toast. There was no glow. I turned towards Miyaanji. His face was glowing. He had made a kill. I remembered his words. He had said, 'It will make the face golo.' He did not say whose face – mine or his.

P.S.: My post facial picture has not changed. The over burnt piece remains as it was. I will stay with it the natural way. Gololess.

The Holy Shit

Recently Sylvester Stallone – the Hollywood Stallion, sent his half-brother to Haridwar to perform his late son's *Shraddha* ceremony, as he felt his son's presence, and was severely disturbed. On advice from an Indian sadhu on a visit to the US, Stallone decided to solemnise the rites for his son's deliverance. Now, this is Faith. Faith in rituals. Faith in another religion. Not out of disdain or disbelief in one's own faith but an attempt to satisfy oneself. Like one takes a second opinion. And, there lies the opportunity for the ones who promise deliverance, peace, success and solace. There is no dearth of such people in India, who thrive on this faith factor. Logic and sanity take a back seat. One is driven by the prescriptions of a convincing practitioner of divinity to mitigate or end the misery that afflicts all of us in different measures.

With the advent of visual media and an array of channels competing with each other, mitigation gurus are having a field day. At certain hours of the day, most channels run Astrology segments where gurus, aided by eyelash blinking damsels, answer viewer's questions ranging from *nikkamma* sons to childless daughters-in-law, the possibility of landing a plush government job, chances to succeed with failed love interests, concern over wayward husbands, finding peace for the family, et al. The gurus have solutions for everything. From wearing a red shirt on Fridays to putting on a turmeric tikka on the forehead to feeding monkeys on certain days and all other sorts of methods, which makes you wonder about the source of such inferences.

As I walk down my society road while going to the office, I hear advice coming from TVs, running different channels with different gurus. I set out to listen to one on an off day, and the topic of that day was what to wear when and for what. By the time the advice ended, I realised that for bringing luck on that day, I was supposed to wear a yellow shirt, red or maroon trousers, a white belt and brown shoes. Thankfully, socks were left out. With my swarthy complexion, I imagined myself as a flashy B grade movie sidekick and dropped the idea of bringing luck forthwith. I then tried another channel. It, too, dealt with the same topic. I have checked up later, as well, and found that the topics on a particular day generally remain common. I am not sure whether the channel astrologers have a Whatsapp group or some other chat app or does this happen by sheer rivalry. If one channel tells you about the right kind and shape of the tilak for your forehead, the others, too, talk about them sooner or later.

However, being a faithful Brahmin by birth, if not by deed, I thought of trying out one of the planet propitiating measures, as I was going through a bad patch. Taking a pen and a notebook, I listened carefully to the advice for Aquarians on that day to set right the patch. The advice was to take two stale pieces of hand made bread, soaked in pure desi cow ghee, rolled and tied up with a red thread, a piece of jaggery with one yellow banana, and feed it to a white cow with a black mark on the forehead. With immense difficulty and the help of some neighbours known for their fondness for stale food, I gathered the stuff and ventured out to look for the described Holy Cow. Hours passed. I kept looking. But there was no white cow with a black mark on its forehead. Exasperated, I thought of continuing with my bad luck, when my driver gave me an idea. He suggested we visit the nearest tabela at Bamnauli village where cows are kept. So, we went there. There were about forty cows of various sizes and shades in a courtyard.

There was a ton of cow dung and gallons of gomutra. I cautiously glanced around. Then, I found the cow I was looking for. Pleased with my turn of luck, I took out the rolls and moved forward deftly like a Spanish bullfighter. But the aroma of ghee had, by now, pervaded the flared nostrils of the bovines, and by the time I could realise and react, one enterprising calf nudged me on my buttocks, and I fell headlong into the heaped-up shit – the Holy Shit. The rolls were being chomped off by the calf and not by my planetary cow, unmindful of my nemesis. My driver was looking the other way, possibly trying to stifle a smile. The bad patch remained. I have since taken off the offending channels – almost a dozen of them – out of my system. I am at peace now. Away from Holy Shit.

The 'Foren' Connection

As I leisurely walked towards home, certain about the showdown with my wife for returning late, Mr Anand peeped out of his flat and called me over for a hot cup of tea. Being a tea addict and a Bong, I could not decline the offer. The showdown was anyway inevitable. So, I wanted to relish life before that. As I slunk on to the plush sofa, Bunty, Mr Anand's son made an entry. He was a young man in his thirties and worked with an IT firm as software engineer, having graduated from an obscure engineering college. 'Hi! Uncle,' he said. 'Long time, no see!' I mumbled something and asked him if he was going somewhere since he was dressed up in his formals. '*Arey Uncle, London ja raha hoon* for two days. Some office work,' he replied. 'You see, Bunty is *Wholly-Solly* in his company and he goes on *foren* trips quite often. After all, he is the Vice-President, bhai!' Mr Anand chipped in, with a glint of pride in his cataract-ridden eyes. I could understand. Having spent his life in a private firm as head clerk, he might not have crossed The Vindhyas in his whole lifetime. I nodded vigorously. The proud father looked a content man.

That night, I wondered. Wondered about the shrinking of the world and about Indian footprints over the continents. The impulse to call even remote counties of England… London. Everyone whose sons were in an IT firm in England said his son was Wholly-Solly and the company just could not do without him.

What was this Wholly-Solly? There is no such word in

any dictionary or thesaurus. Probably, it's biding time to get entry into one.

I, in my reverie, remembered one of my father's cousins from the Banaras Hindu University, who was going to Washington for his higher studies back in 1965. I toiled along with him as *Sancho Panza* through the lanes of Lucknow to buy a Bowler hat, a couple of suits, a large suitcase, and of course a cane. About half a dozen family members accompanied him to the Delhi airport to see him off. What a sight it was! Foreign travel was a dream come true then.

By 1982, foreign travels were picking up. But mostly for construction workers, doctors and businessmen. Frequent travel was a luxury. Two of my seniors from the PSU I was working with in Chandigarh got a chance to travel to the USA for finalising a contract. Their families and they were ecstatic. Suits were stitched, relatives living far south were informed, purchase lists and gift lists were made.

On the day of the departure, they sat in the plane clutching their boarding passes, with wishful anticipation of a *foren* travel. Suddenly, an announcement was made politely asking these two gentlemen to disembark immediately. The department had canceled the trip for inexplicable reasons. The dejected and insulted men came back to Chandigarh to face whispers in the corridors and furtive glances in the canteen. However, one of our officers was beaming for obvious reasons. He had earlier lost the chance by a whisker to these men. He had connections in the department. So, when in late 1982, I sat on a flight to the USA, I was waiting with bated breath and intently listening to all the announcements until the 747 lifted off the tarmac. Then, I slept like the proverbial log.

Nowadays, foreign travel is as easy as going to Ghaziabad from Delhi. Foreign vacations are preferred over costlier domestic options. Europe becomes an extension of Rohini or Pitampura with Lalajis discussing trips to PARAG (Prague), Blake fooreest (Black Forest) or Veenice (Venice).

Earlier, people used to go to Bangkok for a body massage. Now, they travel for an Ego massage. After all, the Sinhas have already uploaded their trip pictures on FB. So, off we go to a costlier place. *Apna bhi koi status hai bhai!*

Career Options

The mucked up AIPMT's re-examination results are out. University seats have been filled up. Thousands of engineering seats are going a-begging. So, career choices have more or less been made. There may still be a few adventurists, who have big dreams, and are yearning to do something hatke. They need not feel despondent. In our great country, one has two very good career options to pursue. These assure us a secure future, provided we have certain basic traits and some back up. These options have tremendous potential to create wealth, immunity and influence. They have many similarities. These options are either 'start a school' or 'be a Baba/Maa' (a guru).

Both need seed capital in the form of land, a setup and publicity. Grabbed or disputed land is generally recommended as no one has the temerity to take action once you settle in properly. In both cases, you need the gift of the gab to be able to influence prospective clients. But such emotive expressions are to be exhibited only on Independence Day and Republic Day in case of school founders and during *pravachan*s in case of the Babajis. During the rest of the time, they are supposed to look serious. Both have air-conditioned buildings with a fleet of well attired females in tow; they usually cast furtive smiles around and whisper amongst themselves. Both weigh their clients by the size and make of their cars, the jewellery they wear and the perfumes they use. Treatment is extended based on these factors.

The basic success lies in packaging your school or

ashram well. The International or Global tag is must for schools. Then, it must boast of excellent facilities such as air-conditioned buses, classrooms, granite flooring, plaster of Paris wall finishing, PVC windows, foreign trips and *Ghar jaisa khana,* as if one is looking for five star hotel accommodation. No mention of educational standards needs be made. For that, the student has tuition options after school.

For Babagiri, one has to initially take along a few friends, relatives, *fukres* and mental cases, make them sit religiously for a few hours of pravachan, during which they are supposed to clap, dance in a frenzy and maro jaikara in a blood curdling tone and pitch to get the attention of the neighbours. Slowly, these chelas are to be replaced with retired, tired, retarded, disgruntled mothers-in-law, daughters-in-laws and people above the law. Remember to be adept at developing a thick skin akin to a rhinoceros, to withstand initial criticism. A few years of this, and one is a celebrated Baba or Maa, insulated from the common people, slowly expanding the business empire of religion. Remember also to ensure that the pravachans convice the disciples that the Babaji or Maaji were present at the time of Lord Rama's coronation or Lord Krishna's Kaaliya daman; that they may have attended Shivji's wedding procession – *Aakhon dekha haal.* The potential is huge. I am witness to a telecon haggling between an established Baba and a South Indian movie czar for putting up a camp for five days. The haggling was for Rs10 lakh difference. The Baba wanted Rs1.10 crore. The czar was ready for 1 crore. This was in 2004. A pretty tidy sum then.

So, make the choice today before the disputed lands are grabbed.

The Bada Gilaas

Years ago, there was no TV. Zuckerberg (Facebook) and Larry Page (Google) were still unborn. As was the smart phone. We had only one source of entertainment – guests. They used to descend upon us, unlike now, without any warning. For an evening, for a few days, or, for months. ATITHI DEVO BHAVA was really in force. Even the dogs enjoyed them – barring some. For us, it was forced relief as the house looked like a relief camp. To locate a shoe or a vest was almost like solving Rubik's cube. The guests occupied the premises like Hitler occupied Europe. And we bore it with a smile. Unlike the present times when guests are not at all welcome, we liked these intrusions.

We stayed in Lucknow, a historical city. Imambaras, the Bhulbhulaiya, Residency and the delicious Awadhi cuisine. Bengali relatives and history seekers took advantage of our sprawling railway bungalow and my mother's culinary prowess. I had to act as guide, and accompany them, year after year, to the monuments. If I had not studied engineering, I could have become a good tourist guide. Lucknow had tongas for such tourists. My place in the tonga was always upfront with the *sahis.* So, I was exposed to the horse 'breaking wind' quite often, much to the delight of the others in the cart.

The guests came in various shades. Some just ate and slept, stayed for a fortnight, gobbling rice and fish curry, and complaining of acidity. They were administered a dose of carminative mixture by my father, a doctor. Some would leave the house early in the morning, to get a first-hand experience of Oudh. They would, however, mysteriously re-appear by lunch and vanish thereafter. Some came for a week and stayed for months. We still tolerated them. Blood relations, mohalla relations, village relations, state relations and their relations. All for a piece of history, fish and gup shup. At times, when the number of persons exceeded the pillows in the house, it was not uncommon to find one tucking (as if reserving) a pillow for oneself right after sunset, in anticipation of the night. When the guests left the house, it looked like a marriage pandal after the bride's departure. But we saw them off with a smile. No one would dare to do it now. Even then, not everyone was welcome, repeatedly. I proceed to recount the case of the BADA GILAS or the large glass.

In Kanpur, two doctors stayed in adjacent bungalows of the railway colony. My father and a Bengali gent called Dr Ganguly. He was in charge of family planning but had nine children. Rab bhala kare. Railways had never played a more sinister joke than this. The hospital where he worked was audited every quarter by a professional from Allahabad. He was a burly pandit with a tuft of hair on his head (*shikha/chutiya*); more than six feet tall, with a girth to match. He wore a genial expression on his face, and like all pandits, his heart acted otherwise. So, everyone remained on alert mode as long as he stayed. As we had recently moved in from Lucknow, we were sounded off about him by Ganguly uncle. On his next visit, my father called him over for breakfast. Puris and potato curry. We had an old Maharaj to help my mother in the kitchen. He started rolling out puris. One after another. And, Chaubeji started his breakfast. He began with a batch of six puris, our regular number. Then, he went on to finish thirty – five puris and a commensurate amount of curry.

My brothers and I, three in all, watched the spectacle with awe and consternation, losing all hope of getting to have our own breakfast, as we took our seats at the dining table most dejectedly. Maharaj brought in some lassi in an average-sized glass. Chaubeji sized up the glass and burst into a hearty laugh. 'Ha, ha, ha, Baccha samjha hai kya, bhai? Bada gilas lao. Iss se kya hoga?' Petrified, Maharaj ran to my mother and told her of the demand. My mother was half dead by then, making puris, and was unable to get a large glass at that point. But one such huge glass was bought in the evening.

Chaubeji had dinner at our place on alternative days, visiting Dr Ganguly, in between. His intake was, on an average, twenty chapaties, a big bowl of daal filled thrice, a considerable amount of curry, and a big bowl of curd. Dinner, the following day, was Dr Ganguly's resposibility.

By 6pm, we were informed that Mrs Ganguly was ill, and therefore, not in a position to prepare dinner. So, it fell on us again. It was later disclosed by Ganguly uncle's Bivishan son that she had feigned sickness to avoid Chaubeji. She continued to do so the next time, as well, until we caught up with her ploy.

Thereafter, my mother put Maharaj on the 'lookout' for Chaubeji's movements, and when he spotted him approaching our house, Maharaj would run in, with the warning: 'Maaji, Bada Gilas aa raha,'. Immediately, my mother would pull a sheet over herself and lie down, as if unwell. By the time Chaubeji got to our main gate, we brothers would have positioned ourselves there, with longdrawn faces.

The man would ask, 'Kya hua, bete?' He might have been thinking about the dinner menu. We would retort, 'Ma is as ill as Ganguly auntie. Maharaj is also unwell.' My brother would add, 'We are going to get food from Station Catering. They make a terrific mutton curry.' Chaubeji, a strict vegetarian, would be aghast and admonish us. 'Arey, you consume mutton even though you are brahmin. Chee chee. Your utensils might have been used for cooking the same. And, to think that I had food in your home. Hare Ram,Hare Ram.' To that, my response was, 'Ganguly uncle also eats mutton, uncleji.' He was quite shaken. '*Sarvanash*,' he muttered under his breath and hurriedly walked towards the Vaishno Dhaba in front of the station. That was the end of his dinners at our places. We brothers were later treated with savouries by Ganguly auntie. For getting rid of 'Bada Gilas'. He is no more but his ilk endures.

Flashback 2001

This was written in 2001. Dwarka was then getting it's first batch of residents. To get a phone connection was a nightmare. To get transport was a gift from

God. Only borewell water was available. Petrol pumps wore a deserted look. Power was highly erratic. Dwarka Tidings was one of the sub-city magazines, edited and owned by Mr KCV Georgie. The article is reproduced for the present inhabitants –ACCHE DIN AA GAYE.

(Heaven. Early morning. Lord Vishnu is reclining on his lounger. Narada brings in a copy of the *The Universe Times*. A free copy of *Dwarka Tiding* slips out of the paper.)

Lord Vishnu: (excitedly) Oh Narada! The Dwarka of my Krishna avatar days. How I long tobe there! Those herds of sheep, cows, buffaloes and great Yadavas.

Narada: My Lord – herds of sheep, cows, buffaloes and the great Yadavas are all there but unfortunately this is not the Dwarka you are thinking about. This Dwarka is a sub-city of New Delhi. A dreamland of the middle class, a land of money for builders and a haven for (co) operatives.

Lord: I see. (Leafing through *Dwarka Tiding*.) Plenty of doctors and schools, too.

Narada: The water is perfect for corroding resident's stomachs and dentures. The roads are good enough to rattle the entire body. Hence, there are so many doctors. The schools are mostly international, fit to be 5-star hotels, as people are fed up with national schools.

Lord: 5-star facilities? But how?

Narada: My Lord, education is being sponsored by parents now. Kids are initiated into schooling on the note, 'Ask not what your school can do for you, ask what your parents can donate to the school.' (No cheques and drafts please).

Lord: Interesting. Carry on Narada! Tell me more about this sub-city. Who is managing it?

Narada: My Lord! They have organisations such as Daily Diggers Authority (DDA), Money Collection Department (MCD), Default Vidyut Board (DVB), and Delhi Jalao Board (DJB), who create and destroy roads, drains and buildings, and whatever else they can lay their hands on, with an alactrity that will make even the Vajra blush with shame.

Lord: And how long will these acts be perpetuated?

Narada: Until another sub-city, another dreamland is created by them to trap the middle class.

Lord: Fascinating! Well I see they have the headquarters of the National Highways of India. So, they must have good roads around.

Narada: Unfortunately not, my Lord. The building is approachable by Anti-National Highways, which are to be named after famous dancers, as one has to dance along to avoid craters, cuts and bumps.

Lord: Oh! Deepak tale andhera!

Narada: Yes, my Lord.

Lord: Call Mr Georgie of *Dwarka Tidings*.

Narada: Both his telephones are dead, my Lord.

Lord: Well, then send a letter to Mr Georgie. Tell him I would like to visit this wonderful sub-city.

(Narada rushes out and comes back with papers in his hand.)

Narada: Here, my Lord. Sign these so that I can send them by post.

Lord: But why ten copies?

Narada: No taking chances, my Lord. Only one out of ten letters reach Dwarka's residents.

Lord: Tell him that I would like to visit the place at night for security reasons. They must have proper street lighting.

Narada: Oh! Yes, my Lord. They have a well-laid out five-year plan. During the first year, they put up poles, during the second, they dig trenches, through the third, they put in cables, and during the fourth, they fix bulbs. The lights are installed during the fifth year.

Lord: Brilliant! And what is the status now?

Narada: Mostly a second year story. But we may plan our visit on a full moon.

Lord: And what are we supposed to carry along?

Narada: Not much. Balm for broken bones, water to drink, candles for lighting, and oh! Yes, some bedding to rest on.

Lord: Why bedding?

Narada: You never know when you will get transport. We'll need that to relax until then.

Lord: Tell me one thing. Are my subjects happy?

Narada: Absolutely, Lord. Everybody is happy, as the telephone is mostly out of order. This means a reduced bill. They are happy and content to pay the minimum electricity charges, as frequent power cuts do not allow them to indulge in overuse of power. They are happy because they have to trudge miles before they get transport. This means physical fitness comes free of cost. They avoid cars due to potholes, craters, breakers etc. This leads to lower petrol bills. They are happy, as they have to drink only mineral water, as no other potable water is available. They do not have to send token gifts on any occasion, as they never receive letters, except for bills. There is no expenditure on parties as no friend of theirs dare visit Dwarka at night. The DDA is happy because it has something to do. The MCD. is happy because it is collecting taxes without providing rudimentary facilities. The builders are thrilled because money is flowing in. Rickshaw wallahs are happy because they can charge just about anything.

Lord: (abruptly) But what about the residents?

Narada: They have to show that they are happy. It is like the Emperor's new clothes. They have to grin and bear it. Otherwise, their friends will label them as fools for having decided to buy a house in Dwarka.

Lord: In that case, tell Mr Georgie that I have postponed my visit for at least five years as my subjects are happy for present.

Narada: Yes, my Lord! They also say so.

Lord: Who?

Narada: Indian politicians.

(Lord Vishnu closes his eyes, and reclines with a smile on his face, which only Leonardo da Vinci can understand.)

On Tension

During my taxi ride from Pune to Shirdi recently, I got to know that the driver was a very religious person. Soon after we left the outskirts of Pune, he put in a CD containing a discourse about 'How to live without tension.' I was attentive as all of us are afflicted with this problem, one way or the other. Soon, I found that the speaker was more concerned about other things – people gossiping, not sitting properly, and the faulty sound system. His discourse was full of warnings, exclamations and sharp inhalations, denoting 'his' tension. I asked the driver to stop the discourse. A man sermonising about the removal of tension was himself tense. It did not serve the purpose. I think about this. Nearly all gurus preach about tension, and exhort us to limit it in our lives, if not completely remove or transcend it. All this, while it is apparent from their actions and deeds that they too are burdened with it. Tension is an inherent attribute of a human being. No one is above mental or emotional strain. It comes to you automatically, without effort. I recount a few anecdotes to substantiate my point. In 2001, there was an attack on Parliament. The country was on edge. Fear subsided only with time. A few months later, I was required to go to Haridwar, all of a sudden, for a meeting. I somehow managed to get a ticket in a three-tier coach of the Dehradun Express. It left New Delhi at night. I got into the coach. My berth was a lower one. The rest of the berths in the cabin were occupied by a family of six.The head of the family was a tall, stout man; very restless and dominating. The train was about to move, and I, finding the opposite windows fully occupied by the children of the family, went over to the next cabin to buy a bottle of water through the window. I inadvertently left my mobile phone on my berth. Suddenly, I sensed some commotion from my cabin. Returning to it, I found the head of the family severely agitated. He was pointing to my phone. 'Whose mobile is this?' he shouted. I came forward and claimed it. 'How can you leave your mobile and leave your place?' he thundered. Before I could respond, he had collected some more onlookers, and ranted, 'This man deliberately left behind his mobile here.

I suspect it is a bomb.' The onlookers looked at me suspiciously and nodded in agreement. 'Kuchbhi ho sakta, bhai. Zaamana galat hai.' Emboldened, the man commanded, 'Please get down. We suspect this to be a bomb.' I protested. 'Why should I? This is an ordinary mobile. Look!' I proceeded to make a call. The onlookers scurried for cover and the man concerned instantly covered his family, as in protected them.

I rang up my wife and spoke to her in Bengali. Call over, I looked at the man. He was staring, wide eyed, even more tense than earlier. I looked like a south Indian, spoke chaste Hindi, and now spoke to someone in a language he could not comprehend. His suspicions stood vindicated.

By now, the train had gained speed, and the ticket collector was making the rounds. There was a policeman from UP with a 303 rifle on the shoulder. This man ran to them and brought them over. He then proceeded to narrate his tale; his version.

The TC asked for my ticket, checked it and returned it nonchalantly. The man was livid. 'Sir, get this man handed over to GRP. Let them investigate. I am from Parliament security and I know these types,' he said. The UP policeman sensed money, and he too, joined the chorus of the onlookers. I panicked but put up a brave face. 'Look here, I am to attend an important government meeting tomorrow. If you insist, I will ask at least a few witnesses and you, Sir, in particular, to also get down,' I said firmly. The ticket collector also seconded my demand.

Hearing this, the onlookers vanished, and the burly man retreated. He knew it was impossible for him to get down, leaving his family. So, the commotion subsided, and everyone went off to sleep. I too fell asleep, tired after a full day at work. The train stopped at many stations. Whenever I awoke, I found the man in contention wide awake and intently watching me. He was restless. He might have been waiting for the inevitable – the blast. Morning dawned and the train pulled in into Haridwar station. Most passengers started disembarking, including the family in front of me.

While getting down, I asked the man in jest, 'You just kept awake all night. Tension ho gayi thi kya?' The glare in his eyes could have roasted an entire chicken. Now, this man, having once being stung in Parliament, was completely tense, which he had unwittingly invited upon himself and on others. He suffered for nothing.

Another time, I was travelling from New Delhi to Howrah by Rajdhani. The first-class coach, where I was located, was attached just behind the engine and parcel bogie. There was one more passenger in the coupe – a Forward Block MP. During dinner, we engaged in mundane conversation. It came down to railway safety, accidents and the consequent insurance. I casually asked the MP, 'Sir, do you know why the first-class coach is attached in the front?' Bemused, he asked, 'Why?' as he bit into a succulent chicken leg. 'Well,' I said, 'This coach has the least number of passengers, collisions generally happen from the front.'

The MP was all ears now. 'So?', he prodded. The leg piece dangled in his hand. 'In case of a mishap, the Railways have to part with only the least bit of compensation.' The parliamentarian looked disturbed, and put away his food. Something was bugging him now. We went off to sleep. The next morning, I found the MP with groggy eyes and ruffled hair, indicating that he had not slept properly. 'What happened, Sir? Did you not sleep well?' I asked.

'How could I sleep after what you said?' he retorted. ' I kept thinking of a possible collision. I was tense with fear,' his tone was resigned. He kept quiet during the rest of the journey, which was, thankfully, short. This is yet another example of how one invites unnecessary stress. He was worried for no reason. He had let a single thought ruin his peace of mind.

There is one more account to be shared with you. And, it might be the best one. This was a chance encounter with a religious person on the New Delhi railway station. It was early morning. I was waiting for the Amritsar Shatabdi to roll in on platform no 14. The platform had a book stall belonging to a religious organisation. I sauntered near the shop and glanced over the books. A monk came along and after having a cursory look at the display, shouted at the salesman, 'Kaisa aadmi hai tum? Display karna nahi aata? Mera book kidhar chupa diya.? Saamne lao, saamne.'

He was trembling with anger and was tense. The salesman, visibly shaken by the outburst, foraged for the monk's books, and brought out two copies. He then displayed them upfront. The monk was not happy. Muttering under his breath, he adjusted the books so as to let the title be visible to onlookers and prospective buyers. It was then that I noticed the title of his book. 'How to reduce mental tension'. I looked at the book and then at the monk. He still looked tense. I asked him, 'Maharaj, are you the author of this book?' He nodded gently. 'Buy a copy. You will like it,' he said. I bought the book and he signed it for me. It cost Rs30. And, it was meant to teach me how to reduce tension. I have not touched or read that book till this day, for I saw the tension gripping the author; someone who was dishing out advice on how to reduce it. The book is still with me… along with my tensions.

So, dear readers, do not exert yourselves to get rid of tension. Learn to live with it with fortitude.

The Motivation

Some incidents change your perspective of life without any major upheaval. In 1988, after six jobs in fifteen years and an unsuccessful stint at business,

I was penniless, jobless and directionless. That year, I lost my mother, who was on a visit to my place in Chandigarh, due to a massive brain haemorrhage. She had come to see my daughter – a month old baby then – from Kanpur. As if that death and my wife's Ceasarean operation were not enough, I met with an accident and badly fractured my left hand. To make it worse, the doctors at the General Hospital, Chandigarh, joined the bones in a twisted way. They did it in a hurry as they had to go for a lunch party and were getting late.

I was experiencing constant pain, and the hand was reset and replastered with the same disastrous result. Life continued. Then, one day, per chance, I met Mr Pai – the then MD of Gannon Dunkerley, Delhi, at the Sector 17 market, Chadigarh. He called me over to Delhi for a job. I met him and was appointed a resident engineer at Guna. I was returning to Delhi by a Roadways bus when the jerks that the vehicle made increased my pain. So, holding my head on the handle at the back of the seat in front of mine, I started ruminating about the tribulations I was going through and the futility of my being honest to an extent of arrogance and defiance, which was bringing my life into an abyss of darkness. I was blaming myself and my creator for the suffering. The bus rolled into the Panipat bus stand. It was still to come to a halt when a salesman

– a stoutly built man with a broad grin – climbed up. He got in with some difficulty, and then I saw that both of his hands were amputed below the elbows. He was selling pens. He sold them with witty dialogues, an earthy smile and a heavenly glow on his face. That he was seemingly content was apparent from his body language. He had taken his disability in his stride and was making his life worth to the best of his ability. He got down after a while, brightening up the otherwise drab atmosphere of the bus.

He left. But he had left me wondering. I was upset just because I had a temporary and curable broken hand. This man had lost both his hands forever. Still, he was cheerful. He had not foregone his zest for life. It perked me up. By the time I was in Chandigarh, I was a charged and changed person. Ready to play the Snakes and Ladders of life. And, I have been at play ever since. With my own dice.

Behind every smiling face, there is a trail of pain.

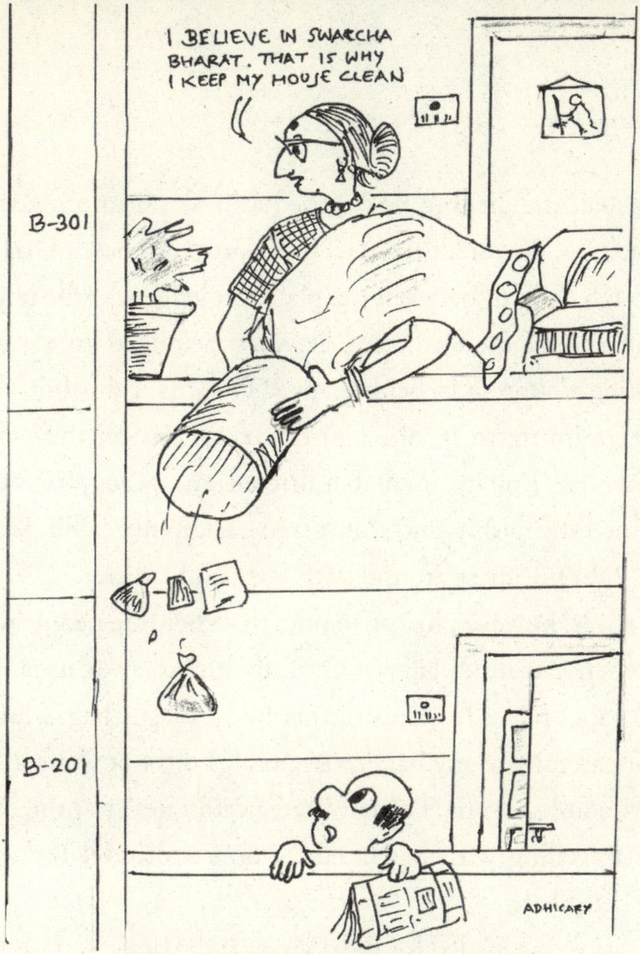

Aswaccha Bharat to a Swaccha Bharat

Last month, I was coming back to Delhi from Bhopal. As the train got ready to depart, I finished a couple of bananas and went near the gate to throw the skins.

As usual, the dustbin under the basin was brimming with waste. So, I casually threw the skins on the rail tracks through the gap between the platform ledge and the bogie. 'Uncle,' said a stern voice. it voice belonged to a sweet looking young lady behind me. 'There is a dustbin,' she said, pointing to it. She laid due emphasis on the words 'There is.' Embarrassed, I muttered an apology of sorts, grinned sheepishly, and scampered back to my cabin. Waise bhi, I do not mess around with beautiful ladies.

I was, however, happy to note that there are people with civic sense around. Later, I dutifully tucked away used foils and paper plates from my dinner into a plastic bag, which I kept carefully in my bag for disposal. I did not want to get reprimanded again. The lady had a cabin next to mine. She was travelling with her family. Come morning, the train reached Delhi.

Everyone jostled for the door, as if the bogie was on fire. I went last, casting a furtive look around, to see whether I had left any waste. Moving ahead, I was in for a shock. The place that the lady and her family had occupied looked like a huge garbage bin. Empty packets of chips, biscuits, aluminium foils, all lay scattered. The preacher had not practised her preachings.

This is the irony of our country. We specialise in preaching but hardly practise anything ourselves. Godmen preaching celibacy and self control often land up in jail on molestation and rape charges. Politicians speaking in favour of anti-corruption laws stack away their black money in foreign accounts. Those hailing women's emancipation themselves do not let their womenfolk lift their veils or wear skimpy clothes.

In the locality where I live, I have come across reputed schools prominently displaying flex boards with SWACCHA BHARAT written on them exhorting students to keep the premises clean. Good move. However, they are blissfully oblivious to the fact that every day, kilos of waste, in the form of wrappers, foils, empty tetra packs and the like are thrown out from the windows of swanky, AC buses, ferrying their enlightened wards. Teachers accompany the students in the bus. Is this the kind of swacchata they are imbibing in the mindset of young children? How about installing a dustbin in the vehicle?

In societies also, residents tend to keep their waste near someone else's flat or in common areas away from their own houses. People spend lakhs of rupees to renovate their flats but hardly bother to buy dustbins. One may see punctured polythene bags spilling the waste on to public areas.

I am stressing the need to inculcate a sense of cleanliness all around, especially in the minds of school children, as they hold the key to the future. A future transforming

Aswaccha Bharat into Swaccha Bharat. Let them be the torch bearers of 'Preach and Practise'.

Until then, loiter in the litter.

This article first appeared in the *Businessworld,* Smart City edition.

Of Vices

The incessant ringing of the phone stirred me out of my siesta. I was not amused at this uncalled for interruption. Contrary to my habit, though it was an unknown number, I answered the call. 'Good afternoon,' Sir.' The voice on the other side was heavenly sweet – as they say. So, I restrained my urge to give her an earful for disturbing me. I have always thought that a sweet voice was associated with a sweet face. Barring a few in Bollywood. 'May I know whom I am speaking to?' I queried. 'This is Latika, assistant vice president – marketing, Seven Heavens Club, Sir,' she said. The sweet voice then rattled away the benefits one can enjoy at their time share units for years to come et al. I was not listening to the matter. I was thinking about the designation she had mentioned. 'So, you are assistant to the vice president?' I asked. 'No, Sir, I am assistant vice president,' she asserted. 'But vice is also assistant? How can one person be two assistants?' I now proceeded to rattle her.

She was unfazed. 'Sir, you are not correct. I will be full vice president upon fulfilling my target. Please join our club,' she said. 'How old are you, my dear lady, if you do not mind my asking,' I prodded again. She replied, 'Twenty-seven, Sir.' I was vexed. Twenty-seven and already vice president? 'Well, beta, does your club "Seven Heavens" have a branch in heaven?' I asked in jest. She stifled a laugh over the phone. 'No, Sir. You must be joking.' By this time, her voice had a resigned tone. I intended to close the conversation. 'See, my lady. I am sixty-seven, and will be up there in the near future. Therefore, I can invest only there. Bye and Best of the day to You,' I said and hung up, leaving her free to pursue her targets.

She made me think. In our times, vice-president evoked the picture of a rotund person, filling up a revolving chair, accessible through a personal assistant, seated in an airconditioned cabin all by himself, conveying his approval or displeasure through grunts and nods. There used to be very few of those in each organisation. The average age used to be fifty-five or so. The times have changed. Now, most young people coming out of B-schools, start their careers as vice presidents or assistant vice presidents like Latika. Thanks to the American work culture, we have more presidents than office executives. There are many variants. Assistant VP, Associate VP, Deputy VP etc.

My neighbourhood is full of proud parents trying very hard to convey that their children (daughters and daughters-in-law) occupy important positions such as those of a vice president in an MNC. Not realising that the status of the VP has now changed. Today, they sit in open cubicles, fetch their own cup of coffee, heat their roti ka dabba, and share the cab. The money is good, but the targets are tough. Many burn out by the time they are forty-five. Some are burdened with corporate diseases. They are products of JHATKA management methods. Stiff, unyielding careerists, stubborn and inexperienced. Earlier, the products were of HALAL management methods. Yielding to bosses, adaptable, willing to change according to situations and armed with uncanny survival instincts. (While Jhatka meat is prepared by executing one blow, making the meat hard and stiff, Halal meat is prepared by slowly draining life off of the lamb, making the meat soft and succulent.) The analogy is that while earlier one had to go through the rigours of office intrigues, staff politics, such other trials and tribulations to attain the post of a vice president, nowadays, one gets to that post directly without much ado. However, a designation counts. In Hindi, there is a proverb – 'Tankwah tees se tehra kar do/naam Daroga jaroor rakh do.' (Lower my salary to thirteen from thirty but name me Daroga.)

I recollect an incident from 1978, when I was posted as an assistant engineer in the irrigation department in Lucknow. The UP government had just changed the designation of diploma engineers, who served under the assistant engineers, from Overseers to Junior Engineers. On one occassion, my junior engineer accompanied me to a furniture shop in Aminabad to buy some office furniture. The shopkeeper, a bearded Miyaanji, sat accross a table, and had only one visitor's chair. The junior engineer went first, and said, 'I am Badri Prasad, junior engineer,' and pointing at me, said,This is my assistant engineer.' The shopkeeper, looking at the aged junior engineer and me, took me to be the assistant of that junior engineer, and offered the lone chair graciously to him while politely asking me to wait outside. It took some explanation from the embarassed junior engineer to clear the misunderstanding; all due to the designation.

As I finish this column, my phone is ringing again. Another unknown number. Another vice president trying to reach her target. Perhaps.

The Frog Soup

I left UP irrigation in 1978 after two years of a bottled existence. I joined the Tata Institute of Fundamental Research thereafter. It had entered into a collaboration with the Department of Electronics, Government of India at Mohali, near Chandigarh, to set up a VLSI manufacturing unit named Semiconductor Complex. BARC, too, was there to extend engineering support. It had a tie up with American Micro Systems, California. Mohali was chosen for its environmental similarities with Silicon Valley.

The facility, on the outskirts of Chandigarh, was planned on a fifty-acre plot given by the Punjab government. The project director was Dr S Ramanathan from TIFR – a well revered scientist – just back from a long stint in the States. A soft-spoken person, he had a soothing presence, and a firm mind. The Mohali of those times was an industrial town in the midst of green wheat fields, with a magnificient view of the Kasauli hills. The project was being grilled in the government tandoor as usual.

Therefore, we engaged ourselves in planting peripheral trees – three rows each of eucalyptus, silver oak and thuja, to provide a dust screen. Dr Ramanathan was a tree-friendly man and his main concern lay in the survival of the plants. There was an old well in the plot, which we used, to irrigate the plants. The water was quite dirty for human consumption. However, having no potable water source nearby, my motley construction team had to take that often. I sent an estimate of a bore well and a filter plant to TIFR, which it forwarded to BARC for approval.

One Mr Krishnamurthy was the finance officer, due for promotion to Chandigarh. He was a sadist when it came to sanctions. As is with many people working with accounts, he found pleasure in dribbling files. So, my estimate was duly buried in the F and F (file and forget) papers. Dr Ramanathan used to visit the site once a month. Along with a couple of officers from Bombay. It was the month of December, and the wind was chilly, when he arrived with the construction consultant, Mr Kulkarni and Mr Krishnamurthy. Accompanying him was a boisterous sardarji – Mr Randhawa – liaison officer from the Punjab government. Dr Ramanathan, immediately after getting down from the car and exchanging pleasantries, posed the usual question, 'What about my trees, Adhicary?' I was ready with the answer – mostly imaginery – 'Sir, we lost twenty eucalyptus, fourteen silver oak and thirty-four thuja – all due to the extreme cold,' I replied. 'What? How sad!' he exclaimed. 'No worry, Sir. We have replaced them with nearly the same sizes,' I added.

'Ah! Good. I am relieved. Thank you,' he said, just as he did each time. Inspection over prematurely due to cold winds, we walked towards the cars. Then I reminded Mr Krishnamurthy about the bore well. 'Oh! That? Let me come to Chandigarh next month. I'll see to it, then,' he said, pompously. Trying to exhibit authority. I was dejected.

Then, I had a masterstroke. I went up to Mr Randhawa, and asked, 'Sir, thand da Mausam hai, chai sai banwaoon?' The sardar jumped at that and immediately agreed. We had a small tea shop. Our Borosil glasses were brought out and washed off their hay fillings. Hot tea came in with matthis. The tea was special with elaichi and adrakh thrown in.

Taking long sips, the Bombay gang and sardarji appreciated its taste. 'Sir, actually this is not tea,' I threw a bombshell. 'What is this, then?' queried Krishnamurthy. 'Frog soup,' I replied. And then, took them to the source of the water. It was the old well, full of big toads merrily wading in it. The water looked like African swamp. Looking into the well, their expression underwent a change, ranging from shock to disbelief. We lost two expensive glasses as they fell from their hands. Withdrawing hastily, Kulkarni began to puke, and Krishnamurthy was furious at me. 'How dare you make us drink this? We could die, you know?' 'Well, Sir, we have been forced to drink this water for the last five months due to your procrastination over the sanction of the borewell. No one has died yet. So, you should not bother,' I said firmly, chewing every word in defiance.

Dr Ramanathan wore a glum look until they left the site. We all knew that it was my last day there.

The following day, a sealed letter came from our office in Chandigarh. I opened it in front of my tense team. I was relieved. It was the sanction letter for the well and the filter, signed by the project director.

Mr Krishnamurthy was not sent to Chandigarh. The PD was not happy with him. The frog soup episode gave him a reason. Till this day, I visualise Krishnamurthy hurtling darts at my photograph hung in his cabin in Bombay. My soup had landed him in a soup.

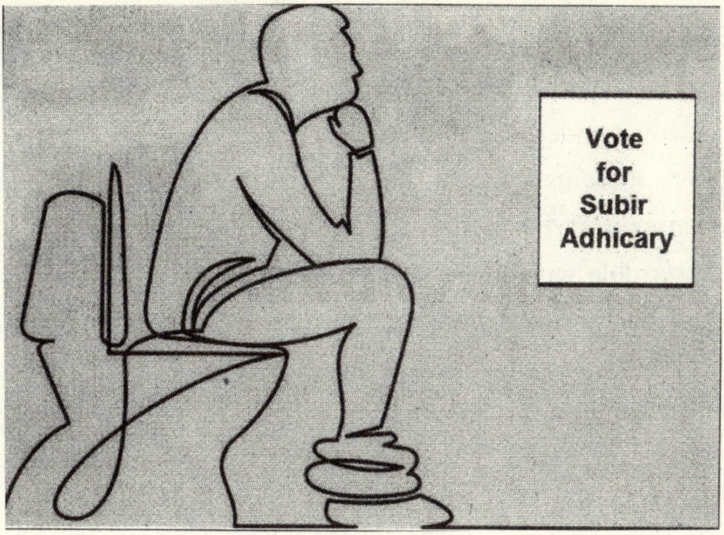

The Publicity Trick

Year 1967. I had just joined REC Durgapur at the age of seventeen. We had about 1,250 students spread out in five hostels from their first year to the fifth.

Two or three months into the first semester, after the nerve-racking ragging was over, and the new students had settled in, the student's gymkhana elections came in. Nearly 40% students were from pan india, taken through IIT competition. I was from IIT Kanpur. Initially, there was a discernible separation between the bongs and non-bongs (called chaaps). Among the Bongs, there were Kolkatan and neighbouring district schism.

Adding to the variety were Nepali and Naga students. So, it was a widely assorted pack. The gymkhana had, inter-alia, a post in the entertainment division, reserved for a first-year student. I was a bong, from Chaap land, Kanpur, and was close to the Nepalese. The masala was perfect and I decided to fight elections. My opponent was a boy called Rabin Das. No one in the college knew us, apart from our small groups. It was, therefore, a fight between two faceless persons. Das, being a common Bengali name, stood better chances. My Bong chaap mind had an idea. The name mattered. It was imperative that the name was registered in the minds of the voters.

The hostels were three storied buildings with eleven wings. Each wing had toilet areas at the end, with five Indian WCs each. I got hold of plain pages, cut a stencil from a cardboard and sprayed paint through a flit pump. The pamphlet said, 'Vote Subir Adhicary as entertainment member. First year'. Getting hold of kneaded atta from the mess, along with my Tom Sawyer friends, I stuck the pamphlets on the inner side of the WC doors, at the eye level of a sqatting person's height. This, I did a week before the elections. For the next seven days, unwittingly, the students had to stare at my name while making the 'tyag' of the day. The patient ones just looked at it. The impatient ones scratched it. The other group tore it down. However, each evening, my gang assiduosly replaced the damaged ones. Over seven days, my name got ingrained in the minds of the students. The morning and the relief made the WC a perfect place for concentration. The result was obvious. It was 70%-30% in my favor. That was my first advertisement coup.

The second one was in 1980. I had taken a distributorship of an adhesive compatible to Fevicol and other brands from my ex-room mate who manufactured it in Mumbai. Being a new product, no dealer in Chandigarh was ready to stock it. I got hold of a few old Sikh carpenters, paying them Rs20 each, to go around on bicycles, approaching the dealers. The question they were to pose there was 'Do you have Vincol? Mumbaiwala?'. The answer was naturally in the negative. Then, the carpenters would show exasperation, and talk highly of Vincol – its price, workability and adhesive power. This created interest among the dealers.

I would then visit them casually after a week – to a flood of queries and orders. I slowly created a segment for the product.

Publicity and advertisement need innovation. They can make donkeys sell like horses.

The Amrit

The attractive bottle of drinking water on the side table in my Vienna hotel room incited my thirst. I carefully opened the cap and drank a quarter of it.

Thirst quenched, like a true Indian, I proceeded to look out for the price of the bottle. My heart sank. The cost of the 375 ml. bottle of water was 12 euros – a cool Rs984, that year. I could have had a dozen beer bottles at that price in our wrongly maligned country. I spent most of the night thinking of the cost of water in Europe. I thought I was lucky to be in India – enjoying natural resources at a reasonable price. I was wrong by yards. Our own DELHI JALAO BOARD (DJB) has followed Europe. It seems as if their officials, having visited Europe, have struck upon a great idea to dissuade people from wasting water. To start with, they have targetted the low voting area with moderately high income Dwarka societies.

The bills raised by them are indicative of the plan. Mindlessly and ruthlessly, they are charging the societies without any second thought or review. The threat of disconnection keeps the opposition to their unilateral actions a dim affair. It is reported that there is no SUNWAI. Pay or Stay dry. The water would be diverted to the vote banks of Pochanpur, Ambrahi or Rajapuri as the masters wished. The white collared federation, with its genuine salvo and concern, plays a solitary flute in the cacophonous cauldron of politics and official apathy. We have an MP, who does not raise his voice, which he can, as the water supply is governed and managed by a different party.

Their failure would mean success for his party. The MLA is not willing to come forward for ostensible reasons, and councillors have no control over DJB. So, where do the denizens go for relief?

Prudence would say the highest court. But, with due respect, they have bottled water on their desks. Free water in the taps. And, truck loads of files to dispose. It would mean a futile and long fight. *Hindustan Times* would relegate the woes to page fourteen, space permitting.

Alternatively, wait for the water table to rise after twenty or twenty-five years, by way of rain water harvesting. Alas, that, too, only if the faulty design of the harvesting pits, by the DJB, is rectified forthwith. For, the rain water just cannot percolate down for recharge with the present one. Just as the advice to change it is not ingressing into the minds of the DJB engineers.

Nowadays, one flush costs more than ten rupees. Or, more. What a costly urination Sirji! Do you pay for it, too, Sirji?

Please provide Sulabh Shauchalayas in the societies. They charge only Rs2.

The Ban-ana City

What an idea, Sirji! To keep our city less polluted. Thanks to you and some kohl-lined experts, Delhi will breathe freely again. Of course, at a cost. With numerous problems to commuters, who have to go by your diktat, Ab aap bhi kya karen? You are a man of words. Once you have made the announcement, you cannot go back on your words. But, you unnecessarily took on the onus to clean Delhi. You could have blamed the neighbouring States of UP, Rajasthan and Haryana for the pollution, as all these pollutants drift into our city year long, without any cess. We all know that smoke from burnt husk comes from Punjab, dust from Rajasthan, and haze from Haryana. In spite of that, you took a brave decision to clamp down on the Aam Aadmi. For, they are your own, and they chose you, over other people. So, there would not be much of a murmur. Good move. Why go on blaming others… like one party blames the others… for all ills?

But Sirji, this Aam Aadmi has a query. Private cars, to be banned, based on their numbers, are about 25% of all vehicles on the road. Out of that, about 20% are CNG based. About 15% are women driven. About 5% are ambulances or patient transporters. Another 10% may be exempted under various categories. So, on a day of a ban, you will effectively be keeping out just 6.125 per cent of the total vehicles plying on the roads. Is the ban worth it? With the present proposal. Just delve into the submission, Sirji, keeping out your well-meaning experts, who have no dearth of vehicles at their disposal.

Now, Sirji, this Aam Aadmi is sixty-five plus, and has to, for a living, go over to Gurgaon from Dwarka, and from there to Noida for meetings. What means would he be resorting to sans his odd numbered car on even dates? How do you plan to compensate him? Your ilk has twelve lakh at your disposal to buy two cars with odd and even numbers but what will this Aam Aadmi do?

You have a long career ahead. So, think prudently before you speak or commit.

All the best, Sirji. Oh yes. One more idea. There is a dearth of schools. So, let the boys come to school on odd days and girls on even days. That could solve the problem.

What an idea, Sirji!

The Line of Fine

Einstein was on his routine morning walk. He walked in the mornings and evenings without fail. I saw him coming with his usual stride – stopping, looking around with curiosity and sometimes sniffing around. Shakespeare was a few steps behind him. They paused to look at me. We knew each other well and understood each other. By then, Pluto also came huffing from the service lane. He surveyed us with bulging eyes in his philosophical way, and before we could exchange pleasantries, lowered his haunches and eyes, which were half shut, as if in ecstasy, relieved himself, oblivious of the surroundings and of his master's apparent uneasiness. Dear readers, until this point, it was a true story. Einstein, Shakespeare and Pluto are English beagles of my neighbourhood. Einstein is the oldest – six years of age. While my pet dog was alive, we, masters, crossed each other, and as the masters conversed on mundane matters of life, the dogs had a great time.

The fiction starts now.

I looked into Pluto's eyes and said, 'Pluto, aren't you putting your master in a position where either he cleans your poop or pays the fine imposed by the SDMC?' 'Really?' asked Pluto, dismissively. 'I know my master. He will neither clean it nor pay the fine. And, don't you think this fine of Rs500 is a little too harsh?' Einstein joined us now. He remarked 'Our masters do not allow us to do it in their toilets. They pat us, feed us, love us but are wary of picking the poop and throwing it out somewhere,' 'Somewhere? Where is this place called "somewhere"?' Shakespeare chipped in, 'That is the tragedy. Poop poop everywhere. Not a place to throw. They want to follow Europe. But lack the infrastructure. In Europe, there are poop collect bins with picking tools on the pavement. Alas, everything is missing in this country, except for irrationality.'

I had a ready response to that. 'Come on,' I said. 'That does not give you a reason to poop anywhere you like. There has to be a change for good,' Pluto sneezed and looked at me accusingly. 'Well. Sire, your Danny lived for thirteen years. Am I correct?' he asked. 'Yes,' I responded, somewhat perplexed. The philosopher continued, 'Thirteen years or about 4500 days, at twice a day would mean about 9000 times poop. How many times have you cleaned up his poop, Sire?' I kept quiet. He was right. I used to look the other way while Danny cleared his bowels. I felt guilty and lowered my head. 'Do not be despondent. Just think of the money you have saved,' said Einstein. He continued, 'Nine thousand times at Rs500 means Rs45 lakh. Even assuming you were caught sometimes, think of the loss the SDMC has undergone just because of you.' The dogs broke into canine laughter. Wagging their tails vigorously in delight.

Then, Pluto said, 'Ok, on a serious note, tell me why the fine is for hapless, leashed dogs like us? What about these Kallus, Sheras, Tigers, Motis, who throng the neighbourhood by the dozens, fed and pampered by all of you? Who will clean or pay the fine for them? We are not allowed into the parks but our mongrel brothers run free, pooping and pissing in the same parks, with gay abandon. There are pet dogs who walk in Nehru Park or in Lodhi Garden, pooping anywhere they like. Is it just because they belong to diplomats and Beauracrats?'

'I say this land is full of canine discrimination,' lamented Shakespeare, scratching his ears. The topic was cut short when two persons wearing lungis emerged from the park carrying plastic bottles. They had just relieved themselves in the bushes. 'Well, well, Sir, who will fine these two-legged canines? Do you have a clue?' I felt helpless. I had no answer. We had tried our best to stop the menace, but the authorities are just not listening. 'I know why,' volunteered Pluto. 'They are voters. There is a fine line separating us.' I stood lost. He was right. There indeed… is a fine line.

The Elephantine Letdown

About three months ago, the residents of Dwarka had a glimmer of hope when MCD elections were announced. The sub-city was full of garbage, construction debris lay strewn over, drains remained clogged throughout the year and cases of dengue and Chikanguniya were rampant. The councillors, who had taken over, just about a year ago, were either disinterested (as the constituencies were redrawn and were reserved for women) or plain incompetent. So, when the prospective candidates, along with their drummerboy agents, repeatedly shouted hoarse that significant changes would be ushered in if local candidates were elected, the naive and gullible Dwarkaites fell hook and line to this Goebbelsian campaign. Hopes of having a garbage-free Dwarka were roused. Long ago, Mr Tejinder Khanna, the then LG, had announced and pledged a zero tolerance Dwarka. It was cleaner, the generation of garbage was slight. Of course, the population was low.

Then came the abundant housing loan regime, and the newly completed societies witnessed a steady influx. Attendant to this, the support mechanism in the form of rickshaw pullers, household helps, drivers, and security guards, poured in and filled the abutting villages – Rajapuri, Amberhai, Pochanpur. To cater to this support population, numerous street food sellers, footpath barbers, tea sellers, and roadside mechanic shops sprouted up in tandem, making Dwarka a fully tolerant zone. Encroachments were all over. Dwarka became like the other neglected areas of

Delhi – filthy, haven for encroachers and infested with criminals. The MCD became synonymous with the Money Collection Department – collecting jaziya-type taxes. This, without the rudimentary services being provided to hapless tax payers.

The upkeep of the sub-city was with another tortoise department – the DDA. Delayed Decision Authority. Nothing moved. The only significant work it has done till this day is to have allowed various agencies to dig up with impunity the superbly laid roads – so assiduously constructed under the supervision of CRRI. The agencies were supposed to either remake the dug stretch or deposit money with the DDA to enable it to do the repair job. No one did it. It ruined the majestic roads. The debris, thrown carelessly on the kerb drains, impeded the flow of rainwater, leading to water accumulation. Trees and pruned branches were thrown about the road berms. Huge amount of construction debris was thrown in the service lanes.

This accumulated garbage is nobody's baby. So, it stayed. The citizens were tired of complaining. The elections came as a relief – for they afforded the chance for a change – for an expected betterment, as promised by the prospective councillors. Dwarka voted normally and voted for the best of the lot. At least that's what it thought. However, months have passed, the rains are setting in, but the much touted 'garbage and encroachment free' Dwarka remains a dream. All the promises have fallen flat. Some cosmetic works and efforts have been made to assuage the feelings of restless citizens but no improvement is visible. The tall promises have evaporated. Not a single councillor or officer makes rounds to check the situation. And, the residents wait for a better tomorrow.

Let me tell you something else now.

During my childhood days, I stayed in DS office colony, Hazratgunj in Lucknow, very near the zoo. During the summer holidays, we, the children of the colony, used to visit the zoo on our morning walks. Our favorite was the elephant near the tiger's enclosure. It remained chained to a large steel hook, and peacefully partook of its morning diet of sugarcane and banyan branches. It was a magnificient animal and we were awed by its great size. One morning, we found the pachyderm restless and swinging back and forth with its the tail raised. It seemed in agony. The mahout stood nearby, looking anxious. We asked him about the cause of the restlessness. With a morose face, he told us that the animal was suffering from indigestion and wanted to pass gas. We were thrilled. One of the 'uncles' in our colony, a Mr Tewari, was a hefty man, with a potbelly. Standing in his verandah, he used to fart. The noise it made was so loud that startled birds flew away from the area and dogs cowered in fear. So, we anticipated a huge sound. After all, the elephant was much much bigger than Tewari uncle. We waited on the sides, shouting and gesturing at other walkers to keep away from its rear. Seconds passed, minutes passed, nothing happened. We became restless like the poor animal, when suddenly, there was a sound, as if air was coming out of a cycle tube – a long whoosshhhhh. The elephant and the mahout both seemed relieved and happy. We were not. We felt cheated. It was a massive letdown, like a Diwali cracker gone moist. Crestfallen, we trudged back home with belied expectations.

I am reminded of this incident when I think of the expectations that we had from MCD.

Fast Food

The media did not have a scintillating story for quite some time. Anchors were on yawn mode and acerbic panellists were emptying out unfinished bottles while awaiting a panel discussion on Jallikattu.

The Monday fast at Rajghat by the now-deposed rajas sent them into an ectastic spin. The fasting team, on its way to a day-long sit down fast, had gorged on chole bhatures. Awww! 'What a shame!' the purists cried. 'It was a mockery of a fast,' shouted the ationalists. 'Tch! Tch! The national fabric is in tatters,' lamented journalists. How could they eat to their stomach's content and then sit on a fast, thought the common man. The evening's prime time TV was once again Arnabian's show. The producers were happy, the anchors pretended to be devastated by the news, and the panelists sharpened their verbal razors and slashed each other, as usual oblivious of what the real issue was. It was as if the country's best past time and apparent show of dissent – THE FAST—was at stake.

The people who participated in the fast – on a full time/part time basis – clarified that it was not meant to be indefinite, and that the binging earlier that morning was breakfast. The overnight fast was broken for another one during the day.

Now, dear readers, think rationally. They never said that the fast was unto death. They are not like the great revolutionary Jatin Das, who undertook a sixty-three day fast unto death in spite of deadly torture to make him discontinue the fast. They never said that they wanted to get rid of corruption and sat fasting like Anna. (It is a different matter that the fast undertaken by the same Anna, last month, flopped; public presence being minimal. It raised hopes that corruption had perhaps dipped. Therefore, no more crowds.)

No fast is complete without a sneak snack, some Parle-G biscuits and a few sips of a soft drink, on the sly. These are fast foods. Chole bhatures are also fast food. To be taken during a fast. So, what is wrong with that?

Our Babas apparently fast for twenty days a month. Their glowing cheeks betray that they abstain from food during their so called fast.

In 1977, the UP-irrigation engineers decided to sit on a day-long dharna, and fast, to press for some long-standing demands. Lokpati Tripathi, son of the legendary Kamlapati Tripathi was the Irrigation Minister with a sinister style of functioning. I, too, volunteered for the fast. We were to assemble and sit in front of Vidhan Bhawan. The dharna was to start at 10am. So, I went to my favourite biriyani corner in Burlington Hotel, nearby, and polished off half a plate mutton biriyani, (all of Rs12) and then, rushed to the venue. There were about twenty people, watched and cheered by fifty more. Some had come from other districts by night trains. We sat on mattresses covered with white sheets. Marigold garlands adorned us, stiffling us with their strong fragrance. A banner, put behind us, carried our demands, with Gandhiji smiling beningly from its top corner. It said, '24-hour Dharna and Fast'. By noon, most of the cheer leaders were nowhere to be seen, and some outstation engineers left the venue, leaving behind their bags, to buy chikan sarees from Chowk. At 1pm. some people came and took our photographs. We thought they were from news agencies, and offered defiant poses. However, the moment it dawned on us that they were from the state CID, half our fasting protestors vanished before one could say 'hello'. Only five of us were left behind. Came night, and with that, food pangs. I longed for kebabs with parathas. My conscience said 'no' to the idea. My logic said otherwise. I read the banner again. It said '24-hour Dharna'. No time was mentioned for the fast. So, guilt free, I rallied one more logical guy, and had the stuff from a nearby stall in Hazratgunj. The starry night and kebabs lulled me into a deep sleep, until I was shaken and stirred the next morning by lathi-wielding, half-pant clad, famished-looking UP police. With the stale garland around my neck and unwashed face, I clambered into a rickshaw, and with a look of a gladiator, rode to Model House. My aunt greeted me as if I had come back after serving a cellular jail sentence in the Andamans. She never got to know about how I fasted. Nor were my colleagues any wiser. For them, I remained a rebel. Without a cause.

The Unreal Estate

The incessant ringing of the bell indicated that there was an impatient vistor at the door. Through the keyhole I saw Mr Sen. My day was over, I thought. For, he was Fevicol on legs. To dislodge him, once he sat someplace, was a challenge. He could talk on forever; cursing and criticising everyone and everything. And, he was a confused man. He was due for retirement, and the departmental colleagues, I was sure, will be relieved. So, I opened the door with resignation. Senbabu slunk in, clutching some brochures, and plonked onto the sofa. 'Sir, You are from the construction field.

So, I thought I must take some advice from you. You know that I am due to retire, and that I need a place to stay. A two-room set would suffice for us. I was going through some flats on offer,' he said, and proceeded to spread out the brochures all over the centre table. 'This is North Breeze, this one is Flamingo, and this, by Shetty's, is The Solarino. All designed by Singapore architects, good landscapes, clubs, gym, What not!' 'So, where is the problem? Go ahead,' I counseled. 'Arey, Sir, therein lies the problem. I saw in the advertisement that the average cost is thirty lakhs, which suited my budget. So, my wife and I went to the area last week. But when we discussed, we found the cost to touch forty-three lakh rupees. The basic was thirty. Then, they added the cost of the facilities, and maintenance for ten years, and some backup charges, and everything else.' He sounded exasperated. So, I requested my wife to get us some tea. 'Tell me the details,' I asked him. 'I am a liitle confused. There are several types of areas – plinth area, covered area, super area, compounded area and carpet area. Just imagine! Five types of areas for a simple flat. And then, they say that the offer can be made on any type of area so that the amount remains the same. If the flat faces the park, it becomes preferentially located. So, one has to pay more. It is the same story for all the sides, only the names are different. Road facing, gym facing, sun facing, moon facing. There is hardly a face left untouched. So, I have to pay extra. For the flats closer to the ground, one pays extra for lift services, although this cost is shared. Kuch samjha nahi,' he said, quite perplexed.

'Senbabu, you are unnecessarily stressing yourself. This is sales jargon. What you need to see is whether the flat suits your requirements or not, whether the materials used are good, whether the water supply is adequate, and whether you like the location,' I explained.

'But you see, the house has to be affordable, too. I do not understand why you need foreign experts for design and landscaping when you have so much talent around here. That is an extra expenditure heaped on buyers. The land cost is uniform on all faces of the buildings. So, why are the charges so much more, on that account? What if I do not want to join the club? There is no option for not having a modular kitchen. Our karahis and dekhchis are not compatible to that sort of space. All these should be thought of to make a flat affordable. Senior citizens should be given preference at the same rates on the floors below. Arey bhai, think about them, too,' he suggested, taking a sip of his tea. He was right, I mused. The affordability gap can be surely be minimized, with thoughtful consideration, while trying to sell off the huge inventory in the country. My reverie was cut short. Senbabu proceeded with his case. 'They said it was a 'Green building'. Therefore, it cost more. But I found the building coloured off white and mushroom, not green. On making enquiries, I was told that it is called green because it is environment friendly. Is that correct,' he asked. 'Yes,' I said, 'and the builder gets some reliefs, too.'

Senbabu jumped at this. 'Exactly! The benefits should be coming to the buyers. Don't you think so? To add to the misery, of course, there is the tax.' I tried to reason with him. I said, 'Senbabu, there is RERA now. The sales will be made only on carpet area.So, you need not worry.' He asked me, 'Oh! So, I do not have to pay for the toilet, kitchen and balcony areas? After all, who would keep a carpet in those areas?' I was stumped. 'Look, Sir, these flats do not have GAO areas, too, like we have in our government flats,' he said. 'What on earth is that? I have never heard of it,' I exclaimed. 'Grab and Own area,' he said with a smug smile. We ruffled through some brochures but they all seemed similar, as if drafted by a common agency. Everything added up to a sum that was way higher than the cost mentioned in the advertisements.

Then Senbabu blurted,'They want us to buy an elephant for pomp, and then look out for its feed all the time. I have other ideas.' He rose up, took a deep breath, and picked up the brochures; a man deflated like General Niazi after the Pakistan surrender in December 1971. Seeing him off, I asked about his other idea. 'I will put the money in a proper deposit scheme, and take a flat on rent, out of the interest,' he concluded, smiling broadly now. Content with his idea, I returned his smile. Not a bad thought, I decided, like the old days.

That is the irony. So much inventory lying unsold just for the want of a few modifications. Let us hope that prudence will prevail, and that the industry will be taken off the ventilator.

This article first appeared in the *Businessworld,* Real Estate edition.

Just Musing

I visited Pune for the first time in 1972 during an educational tour from the University of Roorkee. It was Poona then. The name was changed to Pune in

1977. It was a quiet city with a conservative atmosphere. We visited the Film and Television Institute one evening. We were shown around the place, and later, taken to a big set, where a diploma film was being shot. Shabana Azmi was the lead actress. We were not impressed with her Plain Jane looks, and and wrote her off instantly. She was throwing her weight around the sets. We failed to see the impact she was to make in the coming years; art films were not around those days. Looks are indeed deceptive. We went around Shaniwar Wada – a fort in the heart of the city, and one of the most haunted places in India. It is said that one could hear someone crying – 'Kaka, mala vachva' (Save me, uncle), and running in the corridors of the fort, at night.

A few centuries ago, a crown prince was murdered in a palace intrigue, and he ran around, shouting for help from his uncle, who, unfortunately, was part of the conspiracy. By 1972, this nerve centre of social reforms, and of the fight for freedom of western India, led by Gokhale and Tilak, saw rapid industralisation and the automobile sector flourished, with inbound migration.

My annual visits to Pune started in 2005 after my son moved in. I have been watching the city grow into a cosmopolitan, liberal one, over the years. After 1990, the IT revolution ushered in a new breed of citizens. Intelligent, bright and rich, they brought in a new flavour to the culture and ethics of the old city. People from all over the country arrived here, sending real estate prices soaring, and expanding the city on all sides. Vada pao, Dabeli, Bhakarbari, Misal and other local delicacies gave way to burgers, pizzas, samosas and dosas. Multiplexes displayed Hollywood and Bollywood posters, replacing the Marathi ones. In short, the city has become another cosmopolitan conglomerate, with a tall skyline, decaying values, low ethics and land sharks.

While I stand at a neighbourhood chowk and sip a cutting tea (half a chaay, in a small glass), I start ruminating about the similarities of Pune with Dwarka. The area is full of societies with gated compounds manned by security personnel from UP and Bihar; poorly paid and untrained, as in Dwarka. Management committees are as helpless and rough as in Dwarka.Tanker water is the main source of water supply. Hotels and fast food joints catering to the young, urban office-goer do brisk business. Chain snatching incidents have started. Autos charge as per their whims. Young couples frequent the markets hand-in-hand after a tiring office schedule. Property dealers dot the area. Land mafias rule the rates and terms.

The similarities end here. While Dwarka has a sizeable elderly population, with flats bought from the retirement corpus, here, it is the other way around. IT money has enabled the young to afford and own flats. Their proud parents come from all over the country, gloating at the success of their sons and daughters – products of engineering colleges that are mushrooming all around. They come during the vacations or to do baby sitting, and carry back success stories of their kids, to be shared with their people back home. One remarkable difference is that Pune doesn't suffer because of the lecherous looks of wayward men or from bike gangs, as in Dwarka, and women can feel safe at all times. There are no screeching police vehicles, alerting criminals to hold or scamper, and no traffic constables to issue challans. For, people abide by the laid laws and rules to a great extent. It is cooler in Pune than it is in Delhi. The same is the case with the temperament there.

Yet, with the decaying ethics and culture, the conservative old city Puneites are now crying, 'Deva, punecha vachva!' (God save Pune!)

Stray Talks

A few weeks ago, I came across an interesting news item. A lady in the upscale Jorbagh area buried a rat, bedecked with flowers. The rat had been killed by her pet dog, and feeling guilty, she accorded the rodent a decent burial. It was an uncommon gesture, but it reflected that some of us still have some compassion left. Every living creature has the right to live.

I remember that while living in Janakpuri, I used to take rats trapped in our mousetrap to my office area in Defence Colony and release them near the big drain flowing through the area. It ensured them a hunting ground, as a lot of left-over food was thrown away by the kothiwallas there. The rats must have been blessing me.

I love animals. They give you a lot, without asking for anything in return. I lost my pet, Danny, a Lhasa Apso, after thirteen years of companionship. His 'departure' has left me devastated. I had been keeping pets since childhood but have now decided not to, due to the age factor. Instead, I have developed a friendship with the stray dogs around my society. They are a cheerful lot. My late father used to tell me that the mindset and action of stray dogs in any area reflected the mindset of the residents of that area. Skinny and edgy dogs indicated that the people around were not friendly or open minded, and healthy, cheerful dogs indicated that they were in the midst of friendly and kind people. So, I used to look around for the strays to ascertain this point. I have found it to be more or less true. The dogs adopt the attitudes of their masters. They behave like them. One should observe the dogs walking with their masters.

A slow and brooding walker would have a sluggish dog in tow. A stern and scowling master might have an alert and pacing dog with him, and so on and so forth. One of my neighbours was a retired colonel. He walked straight, and with long strides. His German Shepherd also walked stiff. Another person was a rabble rouser, always picking up fights; his dog was also snappy and unpredictable.

The semi-impoverished strays of Janakpuri, a colony of retired government Employees, always pining for the riches that they never had, cool themselves under tree shades in small groups. They do not bark at small cars like the Santro or the Zen but snap viciously at the big cars. 'Attitude dikha raha hai, saala.' While in Defence Colony, an upscale area, well fed, stout strays stroll and rest seperately. No social mixing except for the occasional wag of tails among themselves to acknowledge each other. They would not bat an eyelid if a Mercedes or a BMW passed by. But the moment a small car passed, they would run after it. Strays from places such as Mangolpuri, Trilokpuri, and Pushta move around the lanes in a group. Although skinny and full of maggots, they display aggression and dare devilry. However, they retreat quickly, with their tails tucked in, at the slightest show of force. Lastly, the strays of Delhi's border area, well cared for and indulged, lie stretched on the forecourt lawns for hours. They seem lethargic and laid back. But if a clan member is poked, they all pounce together, and get the offender running for its life.

Dear readers, please observe the strays around your place. They reflect you. Please be kind to them. For, as Swami Vivekanand said, 'The one who serves the living, serves God.'

Name Dropping

Last week, I was having coffee with one of my clients. We were discussing visiting cards. He had several cards in his pocket. Cards belonging to corporate leaders, highly placed government officials, doctors. It was not unusual, as he is also a reputed builder, and an alumnus of a prestigious school in Delhi, giving him proximity to the city. Delhi Coffee over, I proceeded to leave. He handed me a card. It belonged to an influential member of Parliament of Delhi. I read the card details and gave it back to him. 'No, no, keep it, sir. You may need it some time,' he said, returning the card to me. I agreed. Delhi is famous for name dropping. I thought it might come in handy to flash at a traffic policeman or during a locality panga.

The first thing people do after any vehicular collision is to take out the mobile and call up the local MLA, MP or people who matter, loudly, in front of others, to instill respect and fear. Then, the hapless traffic policeman weighs which of the colliders has the mightier connection. The offence booking depends on that. No other country excels India in selfies with politicians. These selfies are later used to get some respect, owing to such proximity. Delhites enjoy flaunting their connections. 'Oh, Bhaiji to samajh lo ghar da banda hai. Ikk phone, aur kaam ho gaya samjho,' someone will say. The listener is awestruck. People bank on connections as conduits to making a living.

Once, while coming back from Kanpur, a young man boarded the train at Ghaziabad. It was supposed to be a reserved air-conditioned compartment. However, it got filled up with daily passengers. I, too, had to reluctantly let the young man in safaris, sit on my berth. We struck up a conversation. He was a suave talker. We listened to him in rapt attention as he proceeded to tell us that he works in the Home Ministry. The mere mention of this evoked awe in the listeners around him. As the young man began describing the daily routine of ministers and secretaries, I thought that I must get his mobile number, so that I, too, may exhibit proximity to the ministry. By this time, he was effusive over his role there.

'I need not seek permission to enter the Hon'ble Minister's room or any Secretary's room. In fact, they look relieved when they see me,' he announced. 'I fix their problems. What to say, Sir, if I take leave, and the problem re-occurs, an official car is send to collect me so that I can solve it,' he boasted. This man must be in a senior position in the ministry. Perhaps, he is from RAW or some Intel agency. That is why he is travelling by this train, to keep a low profile. Or, so I thought.

The young man continued, 'Of course, sometimes the Hon'ble Minister gets rough with me when I am late in responding to his call. But, you see, Sir, it is part of our job. One has to keep a cool mind.'

By this time, the train had slowed down at Tilak Bridge, and the young man stood up to disembark. 'Nice meeting you all, Sirs. Have a good day,' he said.

Mustering courage, I asked, 'Your name, Sir, and designation and department?'

'Just ask for Rakesh – the A/C Mechanic. I am there all the time,' he replied. That was when it struck me . He was, all along, talking about the air-conditioning problems. And, I took him to be an intelligence agent.

Since then, I have dropped the idea… of name dropping.

Pakora Tales

I love pakoras. The mere sight of the ethereal culinary creation makes me drool. My mouth fills up with saliva in anticipation of devouring a hot pakora. I am pretty sure that this trait is common to the vast multitude all across India. Pakora is our national snack. It is, however, discouraged by dieticians and doctors alike, who paint it a calorie devil; out to upset one's stomach, liver and heart. The kidneys are mercifully spared. Notwithstanding a major bypass and subsequent stenting, I gorge on pakoras. Zindagi na milegi dobara.

A pakora stall has done brisk business since 1963, bang opposite the Kanpur Railway Station. It was run by a one-eyed man called Sri Kishan. Most evenings, we ate hot pakoras at the stall. Golden, steaming hot potato, onion, cauliflower pakoras with hot chilli chutney, whose burning effect lasted until the next morning. Seated on a wooden stool in front of a big cauldron of boiling oil, the pakora maker, with amazing dexterity, aided by his son, scooped out the delicacy, much to the delight of the patiently waiting crowd. He is long dead, but the shop is not. His son makes them now with the same texture and taste, albeit, on a cart.

I met him a couple of years ago. He has a three storied house, and a van to bring his stuff. Pakoras have been a boon for the family. I also fondly remember a Santhal couple selling pakoras near our hostel in Durgapur. Their pakoras, after being fried in highly recycled oil or mobil, were of a dark colour but had a tangy crispness difficult to resist. They sustained themselves on their earthly pakora business. Nearer home, we have the Sarojini Nagar Pakorewala, with a huge turnover. These are some of the most successful Pakorawalas dotting the country.

Therefore, I am amused to find the mention of pakoras on TV debates, in Parliament, on social media and in newspapers. This alternate lucrative vocation is being looked down upon, protested and despised. In fact, when I got a supplementary in Mathematics in my Intermediate examination, I thought of giving Sri Kishan some competition by opening up my own pakora shop with my own man Friday, Raghunath, who, like the loyal Sancho Panza, gleefully agreed, and then, like Mir Jafar, spilled the idea to my mother, who put an end to my yet to be launched start-up even as it was being conceived. I joined engineering much to my dismay. The missing empire still haunts me. Therefore, I was ecstatic when I heard that engineers, doctors, MBAs, lawyers are being exhorted to open up pakora stalls to beat unemployment. Alas, the prodding came late. I have missed the bus.

I imagined the new style pakora shops run by different professionals. Readers may have their own ideas.

1. Engineering Pakoras – The Pakoras would be of the same dimensions. The filling would be cut into square, rectangular, circular, hexagonal or rhombus

sizes. Batter would have defined water-flour ratio depending on ambient temperature. Quality would be checked at all stages and the rejected ones would be kept for internal consumption.

2. Medical Pakoras – The fillings would be tested for Potassium, Calcium and Oxalate contents before being mixed to the flour coating under antiseptic conditions. All fried material would undergo Lipid tests and Uric acid test. A board would display the name of the partner nursing home in case a client develops problems after hogging. Treatment here will come at a discounted rate.
3. Management Pakoras – The filling may come from any source but the cover has to be immaculately mixed. The pakoras would be fried to an exact colour and texture and would come in environment friendly packs of six. Seasonal discounts and on-line discounts would be extended. There would be promotional events pan-India and the pakoras would be endorsed by Bollywood and Page 3 celebrities. SOP (standard operating procedures) would be followed.
4. Legal Pakoras – May come in assorted sizes and colours. The buyer would be confused about the fillings but the pakoras cannot be exchanged at any stage. Payments in advance. Read the duly notarised sale letter before

> purchase that would state, inter-alia, that the onus of consequential medical or mental complications arising out of consuming the eatables would solely or severally rest upon the partaker and not the seller.

Waiting for the stalls. As investments for acquiring degrees run into lakhs of rupees, be prepared to pay the equitable price for the pakoras.

Looking forward to a fried Bharat.

Paap and Punya

1954 – The year of the Kumbh mela at Prayag. My father was posted as a medical officer in the Lucknow DRM office. The lawns of the office were teeming with sadhus en route the mela. A huge makeshift camp was set up to house them. We had a Nepali servant – Manwar, who was a good singer. His favourite song was '*Maine chaand aur sitaron ki tamanna ki thi*' so soulfully sung by Mohammad Rafi sahib. He got attracted to the bhajans the sadhus sang, and one fine morning, he tried to fufill his *tamanna,* and vanished with one of the groups.

No issues. But, the problem was that my mother was in Kolkata during that time, and eight of my father's aunts, mostly widows, along with an attendant, were coming to Lucknow from Dhanbad to go to Allahabad. So, we needed a cook. No one was available. One Michael Masih, a converted Christian used to come over to bake cakes at our place. He had a son named Edwin. Michael, upon hearing my father's dilemma, offered Edwin for the household works. My father was in a quandary. The aunts were (pure) vegetarians and partook food only from Brahmins. Edwin was a Christian. If the aunts came to know about it, my father would have been crucified and ostracised. But there was no other way. So, my father asked Edwin to say that his name was Arvind. Arvind Misra. Very close to Edwin Masih. The gang of aunts came, stayed over for a week, gleefully gobbling the food cooked by Edwin Masih. They were overboard with praise for the ever smiling Aurobindo. Not aware of their inadvertent indiscretion. They went to Allahabad for the holy dip showering Aurobindo with hearty blessings.

My mother, upon return, was aghast. Frightened with the prospect of the wrath and curse of the pious widows, she accosted my father in trepidation, and reminded him about the sin he had committed.

My father replied, 'All human beings are equal. If I have commited a sin, by providing food and rest, then, so be it! Anyway, if they have faith in Ma Ganga, she will absolve them of their inadvertent sins.'

During that particular Kumbh Mela, a big stampede took place. Many piligrims lost their lives. The aunts returned safe, though. My father was vindicated.

Edwin – aka – Aurobindo stayed with us for seven years until my father got him a railway job. He is still around – no *paap* has even scratched him.

It is the intent that counts. Not man-made boundaries.

In Search of Swacchata

The much-hyped and displayed Swacch Bharat mission's negligible response is reflected in a much touted sub-city of Delhi. Dwarka is strewn with garbage, construction waste and muck. And, the city is supposed to be home to well educated, higher middle-class denizens.

The elections for the municipal councillor evoked some expectations but the situation has worsened after that. The apathetic, nonchalant approach of the elected member has emboldened garbage throwers, and they are on a rampage, dumping the waste all over the sectors, with the hapless residents bearing all the stink and filth stoically.

Though the main construction in most sectors has reduced, the extensions being carried out by societies and home renovations are generating tonnes of construction debris, which is being dumped at the nearest open spaces or kerbs of service lanes.

The blame cannot be entirely put on the people doing this but also on the residents, who proclaim themselves to be sensitive and responsive to the issue, and express anguish and anger over this. But only on Whatsapp and Facebook. They have neither the time nor the inclination to come out of the confines of their air-conditioned spaces and fight on the streets. We spend several lakh rupees to decorate and renovate our flats but never care to see where the contractor dumps the debris. To generate debris is our job, to dispose it properly is someone else's.

Our thinking of swacchata is limited to our covered area, not beyond that. So, we conveniently throw empty packets of chips, ice cream cups and empty pizza boxes into the shaft or in anywhere in the society. 'Arrey, sweeper hai na, bhai'. Schools put up banners exhorting kids to make Bharat swacch but their buses throw out kilos of empty cartons, everyday, on the road. Markets throw their rotten vegetables, boxes, and fruits, creating a foul smell in the neighbourhood, and all we say with a handkerchief on our nose is, 'Bhaisaheb, bahut bura haal hai'. No action. Only reaction. This is the irony of a high middle-class area. We have generals aplenty but no foot soldiers to fight. There is one gentleman in our neighbourhood, who had lived in Europe for a few years. He has a Labrador as a pet, and we come across each other during his morning walk. His favorite line is: 'Boss, iss country ka kya hoga? Koi civic sense hi nahi hai.' His dog would, by then, poop on the roadside, and the gent would act as if he had not seen him pooping. For him, that is no civic sense.

A few Societies, across mine, put up Swacch Bharat banners from time to time. But they clean up their frontyard and dump their garbage across on paved pathways, much to the discomfort of the walkers. One of them belongs to a leading public sector, which spends a huge amount on Swacchata, ostensibly, to appease the netas, as CSR.

They are oblivious of PSR – Personal Social Responsibilty. Letters, requesting that they shift the garbage, having failed, we decided that 'we' have to keep our complex clean. This sums up our attitude to the problem. 'Chacha, apna bacha'.We do not stop a trolley throwing deris, if it is not in our area. For, 'main kyoun panga loon?'

Swacchata will happen only if we feel bound to make it happen, not because Amitabh Bachchan is advocating it in a three minute film. The money spent on that advertisement could have easily been used to clean Dwarka. The place really needs that now.

The Bermuda Tangle

Schools have reopened after the summer vacations. People are back from their holidays. The wardrobes are boasting of new designs. Parents are flaunting their design collections to each other while dropping and picking up their children from school, and while they speak of how they loved the South African safari or the tulips of Holland or at least some *Maika* tales. One familiar outfit is, however, missing from the scene: BERMUDAS. Last year, through various advisories, certain schools had cautioned and requested parents not to come in extreme casual dresses like nighties, maxies and Bermuda shorts. It was stated that these dresses lack decency and encourage indiscipline. Poor Bermudas. Perhaps, the school authorities are blissfully unaware that Bermudas are slowly taking over as the national dress of India.

One finds them everywhere. Shopping malls, cinema halls, airports, local markets, and where not, except for a few high nosed clubs and institutes. Yuppies, Mundus, Antels (intellectuals), Vagabonds. Name anyone, and you will find them swarming in formidable Bermudas. People come to meetings, gatherings, mournings in this cool attire. A hot favorite in this hot country. Who cares whether one has Corinthian or Doe type legs? Each one to their own.

If Mrs Walia with her garbled and hairy legs can wear it, why not Mrs Satpathy? That is the logic. It is, nowadays, a 'must must' piece of clothing when one goes on a 'FOREN' trip. One can see shivering tourists along the banks of the Seine, the Danube or the Thames, getting clicked for Facebook uploads in these Bermudas.

I am reminded of a morning in Chandigarh, some decades ago, looking for a flat on rent, with my wife and son. After looking at a few flats, we saw a board displaying a 'vacant' sign in Sector 36, a sector dominated by retired armymen. The house belonged to a Col Chaddha. It was an imposing three storied house. I parked my scooter and rang the ground floor bell. A few African students came down the stairs, chatting as they passed us by. They were all in Bermudas, with their hairy Roman pillar like legs. After a few minutes, a young boy in his twenties opened the door, and greeted us. He was in a t-shirt and Bermudas. He beckoned us in and we settled on a huge sofa. As we sat, admiring the war trophies on the mantle, a girl came in with glasses of water and a measured smile. She, too, was in Bermudas. The brother and sister duo sat on the opposite sofa, and a mundane conversation began.

This was disrupted by a booming 'Hi' that came from a huge person with a handlebar moustache and a cheerful disposition. He was the owner of the house. He began asking me about my occupation, family etc. He wore a t-shirt and Bermudas. Shortly, a fat lady, with kilos of extra fat hanging from all parts of her body, joined in morosely, and started eyeing my wife, an ultra thin lady, with a sigh. It could have been envy or pity. I am not sure. However, even this lady had a loose shirt and Bermudas. By now, we were startled at this display of legs by the entire family and tenants. Bermudas were quite uncommon those days. And we Bongs did not have the courage or audacity to savour and admire the show. My wife was restless and feigned complete attention upon our son. I was also uncomfortable. The interview went on till the colonel stood up to call his mother – Biji, to introduce us to her. I visualised the octogenarian in a t-shirt and Bermudas, and felt a shudder run down my spine at the prospect of such visual punishment. I made up my mind, and picking up my son, muttered an unintelligible apology, and scampered out of that 'Bermuda House'. We still enjoy the flashback.

P.S.: Kuala Lumpur, July 6. Two elderly siblings were prohibited from entering the Ipoh city council building for wearing Bermuda shorts that violated the local dress code. Some were given towels to cover their legs by security men. (*Malay Mail* online). Oh Bermuda! What a tangle!

Deletitis

I am afflicted with Deletitis, a new word, vying to be entered in the medical lexicon. It makes our thumb swell like bottle gourd due to the continuous process of deleting mobile messages. Hardly had the Christmas greetings from all subsided that the New Year messages started pouring in. It is so heartening and perplexing at the same time to get messages from people you have hardly met that you instantly reciprocate lest they send a follow up message.

I have 765 contacts, including sundry ones such as the odd handyman I may have bumped into – Munna painter, Rafiq mechanic, Sharma carpenter. It takes hours to recollect the said individual. The tragic part is that the messages are long winding, laced with all kinds of flowers, verses, religious counsel etc and ending with the inevitable 'Happy New Year' wish. I am not sure whether New Years have been happier in the post-mobile era compared to the pre-mobile years. But I am sure that most of these lack a personal touch, and warmth and intent. They are too mechanical and shallow. Sometimes, one receives four or five messages, sometimes from the same person. A quintal load of messages, taking days to delete. By the time the ones about the new year ones are deleted, those regarding Holi start rolling in. God help us.

With swollen but folded thumbs, I regret that I will be off social media for a few weeks, tending to Delititis.

AAP(Aam Aadmi's Predicament) paani paani paani

Well! AAP's AK-67 has virtually wiped out all from Delhi's political battlefield and the party has attained unthinkable majority, according them.

But, as an Aam Aadmi of Dwarka, I shudder. I shudder at the very thought of the trailer presented to us by AAP's brief brush with power last time. Dwarka, as we all know, is modern day Tughlaqabad, with many Tughlaqs, to be blamed. Bereft of ground water or piped water, it faces imminent collapse. Year after year, political parties and their boisterous leaders have been promising water to the rusting pipes and thirsting throats. Scarcity leads to the emergence of the mafia. Dwarka societies were being fed by private tankers, their high price, notwithstanding.

Calling it a nexus between the water mafia and the DDA, AAP cracked down on these tankers during its first regime, without offering any viable alternative source of supply. This resulted in midnight supplies in a truncated manner at exorbitant rates. Then, AAP packed its bags and left as quick as it came. The tankers returned, at higher rates, but, to the relief of the residents.

Then, Acche Din aa gaye. Rhetoric renewed our dreams of enough water. Dwarka was to receive forty MGD of water from Haryana. Everyone scampered to take credit. However, nothing came in, except for false promises. Various forums, notably the Federation Of CGHS, held protests, defying section 144, and facing prolonged legal action. Water, still, was far from Dwarka.

The victory of the BJP in Haryana, Modiji's assurances

and the Hon'ble court's directions kindled new hope. Alas, it was all mirage.

On the eve of the Delhi assembly elections, the chief minister of Haryana roared at rallies to release water, oblivious of the fact that neither a continuity of the supply line existed nor did Dwarka have the capacity to store forty MGD of water. It was a charade by the parties on the gullible residents. As the exit polls poured in, Haryana flatly declined to supply water. Tit for Tat. Aur do vote AAP ko.

Now, an aam aadmi like me stares into the abyss of uncertainity. Summer is approaching and the demand for water will soar. What will AAP do? Confiscate all the tankers again? Parch out the residents? I cringe at the thought as does everyone in Dwarka. There is no Bhagiratha in sight for us. There is water but only in our eyes.

Dear Arvindji, Wi-Fi can wait, statehood can wait, subsidies can wait. Not water. And please, for the Aam Aadmi's sake, do not impound tankers until you have a tangible alternative supply mode.

P.S.: Planning to start a toilet paper factory.

URGE kia hai

Last Saturday, I was standing in front of the Gateway of India, watching the waves lash against the waterfront. At a distance, small vessels swayed rhythmically.

Behind me, was Hotel Taj, as dominant as usual. The scars left by the 27/11 attack were nowhere to be seen. Hordes of wide-eyed tourists thronged the vicinity, soaking in the splendour of the imposing structures. I strolled around lazily, fed the pigeons and munched peanuts. Life was pretty blissful. And then, I felt the sudden urge to relieve myself. I craned my neck around to locate a urinal. It was a futile exercise. There was no toilet nearby. I asked the peanut-wallah, the balloon-wallah, the bangle seller and a number of other vendors. But all I could elicit was a mere shaking of head. By now, my urge had reached its limit. I was ready to part with my kingdom, if I ever had one, for the required location. I looked along the walls for a secluded spot for a little indiscretion.

The entire length was teeming with people. People eating, people gossiping, people in love. No space for pissful bliss. Then, I came across a taxi driver, who was also looking around; his face contorted, one that would have aroused the suspicion of any alert cop. But, I knew the reason. So, I confronted him and asked him the most important question of the hour. 'Arre, saab, mai bhi to woh dhundhta,' he said, with apparent unease. 'Idhar, pahle tha, pata nahi, lagta hai tor diya,' he noted. Then, he revealed that there was a public urinal about 1.5 km away. 'Where is your taxi? Take me there,' I said and jumped onto the rear seat of the vehicle. The Gateway Of India could wait. The pressure could not. Ten minutes and thirty rupees later, life was blissful again.

Back in our beloved Dwarka, the above incident haunts me. The great DDA planners, while planning shopping areas, totally ignored public utilities. A Few years ago, I had raised the issue of the absence of toilets in the market areas, in a local newspaper. A meeting was held, thereafter, with the then chief engineer, DDA, alongwith the CGHS Federation. The outcome has been the usual – letdown. While the toilet in Sector 10 remains locked and unbearably dirty, the one meant for the Sector 6 market is situated across the road. So, access to it, by crossing the busy road, becomes even more difficult than running to your home, to relieve yourself. The same is the story with the other market areas. One can always notice the convulsed faces of market goers, especially elders. If they look uncomfortable and are urging their families to rush back home, they are… in need.

Dear planners, seated comfortably in the cool confines of your offices with attached toilets, how could you realise the need of public conveniences? I urge you to loiter about in the markets, let the urge get the better of you, and then truly understand your faux piss, sorry, faux pas.

The Patch Work

Whenever I drive on Dwarka's roads, I muse about the roads we had a few years ago. They were truly high class. No potholes, no bumps, no ditches.

Neighbour's envy, owner's pride.

The roads were constructed under the strict supervision of the Central Road Research Institute, and by reputed contractors. Driving was fun upto the Dabri-Palam crossing, Kakrola and the other peripheral limits of Dwarka. The fun was not to last long. Service providers descended upon the long stretches, with pickaxes, shovels, ditch diggers and every other conceivable tool that they could muster. The digging spree had begun. The modus operandi was similar. Dig the road, stuff your stuff, throw in some loose earth, and leave it to God. (God, incidentally, in this case, would be the DDA, who, it is informed, had taken up the task of restoration against payment.) However, God, as usual, does not have the time or the inclination for restoration. Not to be left behind, the DDA (Delhi Diggers Authority, as I have termed it) started searching for its 'long lost' manholes with a feverish zeal, all over the roads.

Societies, in tacit collaboration with officials, dug deep trenches without proper refilling. Now, the main roads became comparable to the intra-sector roads constructed by the authority (the DDA), which can, any day, qualify for Formula 1 racing endurance test tracks.

A single rickshaw ride through any service road can change the geography of your interiors and substantially improve your digestion, apart from giving you loose dentures. (Now, you know why there are so many dentists in Dwarka.) The patchwork that the DDA indulges in, is more pathetic. One fine morning, a few rehri loads of the so-called bituminous macadam are strewn over potholes, patches and cuts, with complete disregard for the established practices of repairs.

I am reminded of one incident from my childhood. One of my maternal grandfathers came on a holiday to Lucknow with a leather suitcase full of patches all over it. The next morning, he got hold of a wizened cobbler and offered him two rupees to repair a loose patch. The cobbler took the suitcase into his hands, turned it around with a bewildered look, and caressed it all over for a long time. Eventually, he shook his head, sighed, and fixing his gaze on my grandfather, said, 'Sir, I will give you five rupees if you can help me locate its original leather.'

I am still searching for the original road surface. Please help me find the same.

The Meaty Tale

Disturbing news has come about of rotten meat being mixed with regular meat in Kolkata and its suburbs. It has caused a lot of consternation. This takes me back by fifty years. I was studying in REC Durgapur. The mess served mutton and fish for nonvegetarian partakers, chicken made a rare apperence. Between our hostel (Number 3) and the main building, there was a big storm drain, by whose side, a mutton supplier used to cut and piece goats. One day, at about 10 am, some of my seniors were crossing the place, when one of them noticed four severed heads of goats but twenty-four legs instead of sixteen. Curious, they went forward, and in the nearby bushes, found severed heads of two dogs.

The butcher and his helper tried to run away but were outrun and held. They admitted that at the behest of the contractor, they had been rounding up and luring dogs, killing them and mixing their limbs with the goat meat. Soon, the news spread to the classrooms, and a horde of students ran in from there, beating the butchers to near death. The authorities shifted them to the hospital. By then, the students had crossed over the highway, to the contractor's house, and finding that he had absconded, ransacked his house, and roughed up the family. Police came in from the nearby post and pacified the agitated students by lodging a FIR.

The matter died a natural death, except for oblique remarks from vegetarians. My roommate was Neiko-o-Zhasa Angami from Nagaland, a hefty boy, bulky as they come. He was, however, unmoved, and seemed content, while we abstained from mutton for some time.

Many years later, I went to Nagaland for a bridge construction. There were no stray dogs. All gone to the butchers. It is a delicacy there. That is when I understood the reason for Neiko's nonchalance.

Much of my memory has been obfuscated due to the passage of time. This incident, however, remains etched in my mind.

The Race

I wait to hear the phone ring, as it used to do earlier. The phone does not oblige.

Years ago, I dreaded the ring tone from my landline.

Mobiles had not entered our lives. The high pitched, incessant ringing used to irritate me. It was not the sound though but the repeated effort of having to leave the comfort of my chair in the bedroom and walk all the way to the drawing room, where the telephone set was kept royally, in a corner, covered with lace. I was engrossed most of my post-office hours, watching and guiding my son go through his studies. The telephone disturbed us. The calls came from my boss, from the work site, and from well wishers and relatives looking for an excuse to come to Delhi on a jaunt. I tried to avoid them all. No after office work, no social mingling, no relatives. I became Arjuna, concentrating on the eye of the fish, which was my son's career. Brighter than the other boys, brighter than the boys in the neighbourhood such as Senbabu's son, Venkataraman's son, Trivediji's son, among others. Therefore, the ringing of the phone became my enemy.

Days, months and years passed like this. We had foregone all other pursuits of life. My wife and I doggedly pursued my son's future. Half yearly and annual exams, joint tests, first semester, last semester, so on and so forth. We set him on the racecourse of life, and we sat in the stands with binoculars on. We watched him running at top speed, in lane three.

'Run, beta, run, as fast as you can!'

'Senbabu's son in lane four is catching up. Run faster!'

'Beat Trivedi! Good! Faster!' Our horse, in lane three, runs; exhausted, panting, but egged on by us. There is no respite until the end. The horses kept on running, not looking beyond their blinkers. They ran for days, months and years. We kept on putting all our stakes on them. The race had to be won. We cheered on. Slowly, one day, you notice that the horses have gone beyond our line of sight, beyond the seven seas. Out of our (binocular) range.

We live alone now. Alone in our small flat. My wife and I. The meagre pension keeps us going. The race has taken away our prime time of life and resources. We wait for the mobile to ring. It does not ring. There is no boss, no site; most relatives have either died or have severed relations. Friends have fallen aside. The ringtone is taking revenge now, by not ringing.

I wait and get tired. I stretch myself out on the sofa and wait for the call from my son, from Atlanta. I know that all of us are waiting. Sen, Prasad and Venkataraman, too. Yet, I live on hope. Perhaps, he is too busy running the race there, too. Or that the time zone difference is an obstacle. Days pass, and the mobile does not ring. I pick it up and dial my son's number. After a while, I hear a now familiar voice. A lady says, 'The person you are trying to reach is not reachable'. How right this unknown lady is! My son has gone out of my reach.

I switch off the phone and try to sleep. I feel a burning sensation in my eyes. I touch the corners with my fingers. They become moist. My eyes must have gone weak. Or, is it my heart?

Forming The Forum

Of late,there have been an overdose of cultural activities in Dwarka. I have been getting invitations to such functions in dozens. I attend some, skip most. CCRT, the only good auditorium, is always booked. Clubs, associations, forums from all corners have sprouted. Some promote their regional culture, some their language but most of them promote their promoters and their families. That is why I skip most of them. As friend Amitav Bose puts it Forum = FOR U (n) M(e).

The reality shows on television tend to bring out the innate desire in all of us to perform like the ones in shows. Dwarka,bereft of malls, multiplexes and other outlets, offers some entertainment through these cultural evenings. However, I have noticed that the audience generally consists of families of the participants and senior citizens yearning for a peaceful nap in airconditioned comfort.

Mr Datta is known to me for quite some time now. He stays with his wife and two daughters in a neighbouring society. His wife is from Lucknow,the city where I grew up,and therefore, she is well tolerated by me. Mr Datta is of a cheerful disposition but looked distraught one evening when we met. 'Come home some day, have dinner with us. I want to discuss something with you', he said. Though I knew the discussion would be gloomy,the thought of a Lukhnawvi spread goaded me to be the earful guest one weekend. After the general gup-shup about the Delhi heat, crime in Dwarka, power cuts etal, we moved to the dining table. The overpowering smell of jaffran wafted along and I was transported to Oudh.

Halfway through my gastronomic journey, Duttaji broached on the cause of his depression. He revealed that his wife was a terrific singer and the daughters were female Prabhudevas. Though many a times he had tried to get them into some function, oldcoteries stalled the moves. Dwarka's cultural field is full of politics, he said. He wanted my advice in the matter and wanted me to recommend their cases to some organisation. He offered impromptu demonstration, which I politely declined as I had polished off the last grain of the Biryani and wanted a second chance of dinner. 'Well, let me think about it', I said and promised to return very soon for one more round of Biryani and for the demo.

The very next week I was there,ready for a sumptous fare. They were ready too. The sofas were lined up to make clear space. The evening would start with dance, I was told. By now I could smell the charcoal grilled sheek kebabs and was ready for any show. The dance started. The girls looked like mini Saroj Khans and swayed to the rhythm of a dance number – an imperfect cross between African and Mexican. The slow beats increased to fast beats and I started skipping my heart beats. Looking at their Gothic legs pounding the floor, I exclaimed, 'Fantastic, awesome!!'. The comments were, however, for the builder whose roof was strong enough to withstand the torture these girls subjected it to. As for the dance,mercifully the song stopped as my kebabs came in and I got emotionally motional with them.

'Now the songs', announced Dattaji with glee. The plural implied that she would sing a number of songs and not one. I was stuck with kebas and was lassoed.Point of no return. Just grin and 'beer'. Mrs Datta broke into a song before I could break into a kebab. She sang and it seemed something between crooning and croaking. I choked on the kebab. She was certainly a better cook than a singer, I surmised. Unfortunately, my effusive praise for the succulent kebabs in the form of 'wah, wah's was taken as an appreciation of her rendering and I was subjected to a long repetition of the antara I wanted to avoid.

'How's that?', asked Dattaji. 'Absolutely wonderful', I was still dazed with the awe-perspiring performance and now I knew why no one took the risk. It took me several dinners and accompanying cacophony to come up with the idea.' Where do you come from?', Iasked Dattaji. 'Gonda, UP.' 'Good,do you have some senior officer in the Govt from Gonda?' 'Oh yes, there is one IAS officer heading Upliftment of Tribal Committee', he said.

'Fine. Form a Gonda Cultural Forum with this officer as Chief Patron. Make yourself President of this forum.

Stuff in a few friends as members. Hall booking shall cost you about 20,000 which you can afford to spend. Start your programme with bhabhijis song and finish off with bitiya's dance. Oblige your friends with intermediate slots', I advised.

'Brilliant idea', Dattaji gushed, pumping my hands up and down, 'I start from today.' I bore the pain of the pumping, in anticipation of more dinners. I am waiting now for one more invitation card.

The Education Minister

By the year 1969, all of West Bengal was engulfed in the forest fire of Naxalism. The student class was the most affected, and educational institutes felt the heat. There were severe disruptions in the studies; bright students joined the movement, and left college, to take the revolution to the rural areas.

Group clashes in the educational institutes became a routine matter. Reputed institutes such as Presidency College, Jadavpur University, and BE College were the hub of the Naxal students, and their exploits encouraged other students throughout the State to take up arms against the establishment. The Regional Engineering College at Durgapur was no exception. Durgapur, being an industrial town, was dominated by the CPI(M). The college was Naxal-dominated. The result was disastrous. In 1970, a student of final year engineering, opposed to the Naxal ideology, was mercilessly beaten to death by his classmates within the campus. The college was closed sine-die.

The college, being centrally aided, forty per cent seats were reserved for students from States other than West Bengal. The intake was through the IIT entrance tests and subsequent interviews.

The students who joined through the IIT entrance exams were upset with the frequent closures, the vitiated atmosphere and the constant fear. Therefore, when the college was closed sine-die and the hostels were vacated, some of them from Delhi, decided to try for migration. For this, the Education Department was to be approached.

It was 1970. Mrs Indira Gandhi was the PM and Dr VKRV Rao was the Education Minister. The parents of some students met the secretary, Education. But their request was curtly turned down. This was the time when Sanjay Gandhi had just appeared on the Indian political scene, having been introduced by his mother to the chief ministers and party men as a person of consequence. A conduit was identified; someone who impressed upon Sanjay Gandhi that he must help the students. Sanjay set up a meeting with the Secretary, Education Department.

On a parallel track, senior bureaucrats were approached by the parents of some students to put pressure. As the students were selected through IITs, the institutes were asked to accommodate the REC students. The IITs flatly refused. They were up to full capacity. Persuasions continued, and Mr LS Chandrakant, joint secretary of the department, was given the responsibility of the matter. As the college was closed before the final examinations, it was conveyed that the students would lose one academic year in case the migration happened. The students agreed. They just wanted to be out of Durgapur. After few days, IIT Delhi relented and agreed to take a few students into the electrical stream. Then, IIT Bombay took a few mechanical stream students. IIT Kanpur took only one student of metallurgy.

During those days, communication avenues were poor, and students staying outside Delhi could not be apprised of the developments. The list consisted of the students from Delhi and Mumbai, and once the list was finalised, the IITs ended the process. About twenty or twenty-five had migrated. Many more were left out, blissfully unaware of the migration, and waiting for the college to re-open. I was one of them. My evenings were spent on platform No 1 of the Kanpur Central AH Wheeler outlet. Sitting on a stool, I devoured the magazines, displayed for sale, carefully peeping in, without damaging them. My father had just retired from the Railways as a medical officer, and the station area was under him at that time. So, I had unhindered access to the station. During one such foray to the station, I came across a batch mate who had migrated to IIT Kanpur. I got to know of the details of the development and of the news that the IITs had sternly refused to take any more students. I was restless and could not sleep that night. I, too, did not want to go back to Durgapur, as my parents were very uncomfortable with the situation there.

I decided to try my luck and and migrate. I took a night train the very next day and reached Delhi in the morning. One of my relatives stayed in Kidwai Nagar. I parked myself there. By 11 am, I was at the Shastri Bhawan reception, where a visibly inundated lady was looking after the entries. I convinced her for a meeting with Mr Chandrakant, the joint secretary, which she reluctantly arranged. Mr Chandrakant sat in a huge office with a big desk. He was a thick-set man with a big round face bereft of all emotion. He casually read my name from the slip that the reception had given and the moment he read the purpose – transfer from REC Durgapur – he signed and returned the slip.

'Sorry, the migration is over,' he said, immersing himself in a heap of files. 'But, Sir,' I stuttered. 'We were not given a chance to request.' He looked at me, and said, 'That is your bad luck. Your friends should have given your names in the list they handed to me. Now there are no more seats. Please go back home and wait for REC to re-open.' I came out of the room and had kulche chole from the nearby kiosk, thinking about my next move. By 11am, the next day, I was again at the reception. The lady did not entertain me, this time. She was instructed by the secretary not to allow any student from REC. I felt insulted. I sat on the bench across the reception all day. Mr Chandrakant came down for a meeting at about 4.30pm. I stood and bowed. He cast a furtive look at me and increased his pace. The following day, I was not even allowed to wait on the bench. A burly guard ensured that I was out of the block.

I went back to Kanpur and thought of ways to influence

the secretary. The MP from Kanpur was Mr SM Banerji, a CPI stalwart. He ruled the ordinance factories and other big industries. He was affectionately called 'Dada' and had a good rapport with central ministers. One of my cousins suggested that I meet him for help. I was told that he was in Delhi at that time. Collecting his address, I went to Delhi. As I reached his flat in North Avenue, he was preparing to leave. Yet, he listened to me and offered me accommodation in his flat. He said that comrade Dange was under detention, and that party members were busy getting him released. He had no time for irrelevant matters. Thereafter, he left in a white Ambassador, along with his labour leader chelas, to attend to relevant matters.

The flat was full of industrial workers from Kanpur. The all-pervading smell of bidis floated around. There was hardly any space left in the rooms. The offer was magnanimous, but the place was hell. Disheartened, I left for my relative's place. Meanwhile, one of my friends, a former roommate from Lucknow, got admitted to IIT Madras. His father was a friend of the 'Young Turk', Chandra Shekhar, from his Allahabad days, and he had managed to get his son a seat through Chandra Shekhar, who, then enjoyed clout with the PM. This news made me more resolute to get out of Durgapur. I stayed back in Delhi for a week, walking along the ministerial bungalows of Lutyen's Delhi to get an opportunity to get hold of some sympathetic ear. I was a naïve young man to even think of that. I left Delhi for Kanpur after a week of idle loitering and failed attempts to meet the secretary, Education Ministry.

After a couple of days, I mustered the mental strength to make one final attempt, and one night, I went to the station to board a train to Delhi. While going towards the ticket counter, I met Shuklaji, a guard, who was my father's patient. He asked me where I was headed. On being told, he said, 'I am the guard of this train to Delhi. You do not have to buy a ticket. Just go and sit in the second-class compartment. In case anyone asks for your ticket, give him my name.' I had about Rs40 in my pocket. Shuklaji's words were a big relief for me. Those days, there used to be second class compartments. I settled myself in one of them and was soon fast asleep.

A few hours later, I felt a gentle tap on my shoulders. There were some uniformed ticket checkers and a few RPF jawans. I surmised that it was a surprise check. One of the TTEs asked for my ticket. I had none to show. He asked me why I was travelling without ticket. Getting a chance, I narrated my sob story, the desperation, my father's retirement from the Railways and my compulsion to travel to Delhi. The TTE was an elderly south Indian. He listened patiently, and said, 'Then, you are doing a disservice to your father by travelling without ticket. He will feel too bad when he hears about his son being in RPF custody at Tundla.' I was petrified. His statement was clear. I was on the verge of tears, when he asked me, 'Tell me, young man. Has any railway TTE or staff told you to travel free? If yes, tell me his name. I will let you be.' His partner chipped in, 'See, we are Nandaji's team. We are from Southern Railways. We are here to curb ticketless travel and end corruption. So, you can help us.' I imagined poor Shuklaji in Tundla Jail, his family standing outside the cell, all in tears. So, I said, 'No, Sir, it is my fault. Please do whatever you want to do with me.'

My resigned look and slumped body language cut some ice with the 'Nanda gang'. ' Then, pay the penalty,' said the TTE, and brought out the receipt book from his pocket. The ticket and penalty cost me Rs thirty-two. I was left with a princely sum of rupees eight. Gulzari Lal Nanda was the Railway Minister during that time and he had deployed such intra-railway gangs to stop corruption. Southern Railways officials checked Northern Railways and Northern Railway officials checked Southern Railways. I became a victim of the 'Nanda Gang'.

The train stopped at Tundla. The gang alighted and moved to other trains. Shuklaji sauntered to my compartment in white pants and vest, stifling a yawn.

'Sab thik thak hai, bhaiya?' he queried, peeping through the window bars. I narrated the episode. 'Did you take my name? Bahut khatarnak gang hai. I could lose my job,' he said, looking quite flustered. I pacified him by assuring him that I had not given him away. I added, that in the process, I had lost nearly all my money. He fished out a five rupee note, saying that was all he could afford to give me. I took that and went back to sleep blissfully, knowing I had nothing to lose.

I used the New Delhi station waiting room for my morning ablutions. I was mentally tired but fired from within. I thought of doing something daring. I took a bus to Tughlaq Road. I had earlier seen the bungalow in which the Education Minister stayed. Time has obfuscated my memory and I do not recall the name of the road. It was a big bungalow on the main road. There were two wooden gates. One was kept closed, and the other had a sentry post, where an armed guard stood. I circled the bungalow. It was around 8am. The sentry looked restless. I could guess that he was to be relieved now. After a few minutes, the sentry moved towards the staff quarters with his back towards the gate. This was the moment I was waiting for. Stealthily opening the gate, I walked to the bungalow, tip-toeing on a red gravel path. It led to a long verandah. A small room was on the right side. Its door was open. I moved into the room silently and came across a person sitting facing the door. He was the personal assistant to the minister. Surprised, he rose to face me. He was a small man, now, wide eyed and confused. Before he could open his mouth, I bid him a good morning, and told him that I wanted to meet 'Sir'. I could see that he was pondering whether this young man with a kit bag on his shoulder, who looked like a south Indian, was related to the minister.

I ignored him and went in to the next room. The PA closed in from behind. I was now face-to-face with the Education Minister of India – Dr VKRV Rao. He was sitting across a table with files and books all over it. He wore a khadi half shirt, and black frame glasses. He looked bewildered. 'Who is this?' he asked the PA. The personal assistant fumbled, and realising that I was unknown to the minister, grabbed me from behind, and replied that I had gatecrashed. The minister was livid. He asked the PA to call the guard, and looking at me, said, 'Why did you trespass? I could send you to jail for this.' Something in me must have exploded. For I blurted out, 'I will be thankful to you for that, Sir. At least, there, I will have food and a place to stay.' There was pathos and anguish in my voice.

Dr Rao sensed that I needed help. He motioned the PA to go and asked me to sit down. I narrated my story to him – the REC Durgapur situation, the uncertain future of the students, IIT's refusal to take any more students, and my father's retired status. While I was narrating my woes, the lady of the house quietly entered the room and stood behind her husband. The minister introduced her, and I, rising from my seat, acknowledged her with folded hands. As I narrated my harrowing Delhi experience and my inability to muster money even to go back, the minister turned to his wife, and said, 'Please get him something to eat'. Mrs Rao went away and came back with a plate of idlis. I could not believe my eyes. A cabinet minister's wife, personally bringing in breakfast for an unknown intruder. (I was later told that she was the then Vice Principal of Miranda house).

Dr Rao was visibly upset at the upsurge of the Naxals and its fallout on the intelligentsia. However, he did not delve much into the topic. Instead, he lamented that unlike in the USA and in other countries, the syllabus of universities in India differed heavily for the same course, and therefore, migration mid-way meant the loss of a year. He wasn't briefed fully by the secretary, Education about the REC migration status.

Now, he assured easy migration for all students, whoever wanted to move, irrespective of the quota. He called his PA and asked him to tell Mr Chandrakant about me. He also instructed that I was to be accommodated in a good engineering institute. A good twenty minutes had passed. I took his leave, stunned and overwhelmed with the treatment. He was immersed in his files by then.

I was a man on the moon. I walked as if I had won a kingdom. That day, when I reached Shastri Bhawan, the receptionist recognised me and gave me a slip for Mr Chandrakant, with due courtesy. I ran upstairs, the peon took the slip in, and summoned me inside. For the first time, I saw Mr Chandrakant smiling. Motioning me to a chair, he said, 'You never told me that you knew the minister.' Apparently, he also mistook me to be related to the dignitary. Trespass was beyond his thoughts. I appeared casual. 'Well, I did not think it proper, Sir,' I replied. 'Alright, you go back to, er !!! where?' he asked. 'Kanpur, Sir,' I said. 'Yes, yes. Kanpur. Leave your application here. Go home and wait for my confirmation.' I thanked him and bid him goodbye. I was still unsure whether action would be taken.

I had a princely lunch for Rs7, leaving me short for the return ticket. I bought a ticket up to Hathras and travelled to Kanpur without a ticket, again. A week passed. Nothing happened. Then, there was a flood of telegrams, offering seats in Guntur, Trichy, Baroda, Chandigarh and Roorkee. The University of Roorkee was the Mecca of Civil Engineering and engineers. I dashed off to Roorkee and secured admission there. We do not have ministers like Dr Rao anymore. He had a Doctorate in Economics from UK. He set up the Delhi School of Economics and two more institutes of repute. A scholar and a politician, he was the Minister for Shipping and Transport before taking over Education and Youth Welfare. Had I trespassed a minister's bungalow today, I would have been eating dal roti in Tihar, and not idlis in a minister's home.

Subir Adhicary is a civil engineer from University of Roorkee (IIT) and works as a consultant. His keen sense of observation comes from his theatre background as an acclaimed actor and director. He is a well-known cartoonist and illustrator and has written for *The Times of India* and *Business World group* magazines. He is also the author of a very successful blog. He writes with equal ease in Bengali and Hindi. He lives in Delhi.

adhicary@yahoo.co.in